Adventure House
Presents

GANG MAGAZINE

May 1935

This reprint edition is a facsmile edition. Variations in print and quality are mostly attributable to the rough woodpulp original this reprint edition is based on.

ISBN: 1-59798-060-9

Published by Adventure House
914 Laredo Road
Silver Spring, Md 20901
www.adventurehouse.com
sales@adventurehouse.com

THE GANG MAG

JACK PHILLIPS, *Editor* Vol. I, No. 1 MAY, 1935

FOUR COMPLETE NOVELETTES

THREE SHORT STORIES

THE GANG MAGAZINE, published bi-monthly by Lincoln Hoffman, 220 W. 42nd Street, New York, N. Y. Editorial and Executive offices 220 W. 42nd Street, New York, N. Y. Application pending for entry as second-class matter at the Post Office at New York, N. Y., under Act of March 3, 1879. Application for title pending at U. S. Patent Office, Washington, D. C. SUBSCRIPTION: Single Copy, 15c; Yearly (6 issues), 90c.

SEX LIFE IN AMERICA
The largest publishers
in America of
privately printed books on
LOVE-WOMAN-SEX
will send you
ILLUSTRATED
confidential catalogues
• FREE •
Curious Sex Customs
Flagellation Tortures
Scientific Sexualia
Mysterious Practices
Sexual Slavery
Underworld Vices
Panurge Books
All Privately Printed
Are Not Sold in
General Book Shops
THE PANURGE PRESS • 70 FIFTH AVENUE • NEW YORK
Please send me in plain sealed envelope FREE
your package of ILLUSTRATED confidential catalogues.
Name
Age
Address
6105
MAIL THIS COUPON AT ONCE!
YOU'LL GET THE SURPRISE OF YOUR LIFE

Decks of Death

By EARL W. SCOTT

CHAPTER I

Chinatown Death

MY brogues whipped from the desk top, struck the floor with a thump. I shot out a hard hand, seizing the insistent phone. I was still full of the black headlines plastering the rustling paper that lay in my lap. They read:

GIANT GEM THEFT ON AVENUE

Torquin and Company lose hundred thousand in diamonds. Two thieves killed in getaway. One escapes with loot.

I was wondering what the hell was coming over Murdock's coppers that they couldn't spike such stuff. Here was the third knockover in a week's time.

I lipped into the mouthpiece, "Yeaha? Brandt Lennox speaking."

A voice snapped in over the wire. It was Captain Gorky at Headquarters. Gorky said, "Get this Brandt. A hot tip just blew in by phone for the Chief. About five minutes ago. Some stool squealin', I'm hunching, on this late gem stickup. Just why the hell he didn't call in some of the boys, I don't know. Anyway, Murdock got damn mysterious, hooked his hat and made tracks out the door. I didn't get much of the conversation but did catch the words Torquin and Lupin Square. I stuck Delevan on his tail but you know that can't last. Drop over, can you, and relieve him. He'll flag you down. I'm hunching the Skipper's headed into trouble again. God knows I wish he'd quit this doing singles in that Chink district."

"Check," I offered, then added, "not that it's any of my never-mind but you know how far the gloved hand business will get with those red-hots. Sooner or later Murdock's going to take a shiv in the ribs, pulling the philanthropist."

Gorky's groan answered, "You're telling me? Now step on it, will you?"

"Pronto," I grunted and hung up.

At eleven p. m. the hot channeling streets still gasped under the prolonged heat wave that kept its vicious grip with small surcease through the hours of darkness.

My cab, scuttling eastward toward the drowsy river that had shrunk to a trickle the past weeks, rolled off East Main into the town's backwash on Oriental Avenue.

There were scattered lights here, sure. Paving such as it was, city water and sewer, but from the myriad of smells gusting from yawning tenement windows off stinking cobbles and out of sweating alley mouths, the Chinks had pretty well forgotten that such a thing as sanitation existed.

Nosing toward Lupin Square, the bobbing cab lights picked out unpainted walls clustered with tiny balconies that sagged with restless heat, haunted Orientals sleeping in droves under the leaden sky. Far ahead glowed the garish marquee of the Mandarin Palace. It was a fancy tourist joint catering to slummers. Aside from one or two such gestures toward respectability, the present half mile was a little Shanghai of twisting filthy alleys and courts backing up to the warehouse district of the North River.

There was gambling, dope shoving, high-jacking and every merry hell behind the sweating walls, sagging stairways and gloomy cellars that seldom saw the light of day. Here was the quarter that for half a century had cankered the side of Center City. Strong-arm stuff was all the Lupinites understood. Riot squads, tear gas and hot lead.

Clattering over the uneven cobbles I scowled grimly into the onrushing night, raking the dingy sidewalks for sign of the gray-haired chief. The whisper that Murdock, for twenty years Skipper at Center City H. Q. was losing his grip, had grown into open talk. Certainly, it was true crime was running rampant over the town. Hard-faced bulls tromped the streets and foregathered at Headquarters muttering among themselves, puzzled looks in their eyes. They had a healthy love and respect for their chief but something was drastically wrong. They waited for commands that didn't materialize, warmed seats in squad room chairs when action was the order of the day.

Murdock had gone soft, but why?

Political enemies howled "graft" to high heaven, but the men knew better. Especially Cap Gorky, old friend of the aging officer.

I'd answered Cap's call some ten days previous, and we'd had a heart to heart in his dingy office. It had ended in my accepting the office of protective shadow to the Chief.

"No use siccing one of our own men on the job," Gorky had said. "I tried that and the boss near canned him. He's taken to making Mission meetings on the q.t. and hobnobbing with the riff-raff on the water front. Got reform in his head.

"Anybody else, I'd say let nature take its course, but I can't forget the Skipper in his prime. The men are taking it the same way and we're all hoping he'll snap out of it before the Commissioner shows the iron heel."

That had been a sensation, getting an SOS from the bulls. They'd been suspicious of my lone wolf trail for years, ridden me hard at times; but in spite of it all, I'd liked Murdock. He was a white guy and a great officer.

When braced for the reason of Murdock's crack up, Gorky'd offered increasing age, an old head wound, and the fact that the Chief had gone extremely religious since the meetings at the coliseum held by a West Coast Revivalist in the spring.

Granting such work did much good, it was hard to believe that the steely-eyed, hard-jawed Murdock had turned missionary, but his actions suggested it. And the hell of it all was the thing had stolen Murdock's punch, robbed him of all caution, made him meat for the first cheap red-hot that crossed his path. He'd spent twenty years cracking gangs, socking leads behind bars, shooing killers toward the hot squat. It was a bit late to pull the glad hand and soft answer now.

Events proved it. Three times in as many days, trailing the poor devil down water-front streets, I'd shooed off furtive followers by the show of cold steel and a ready rough-house. It couldn't last. Some punk would clock me sooner or later and blotto a crack officer who had been the talk of the East Coast in his time.

I snapped free of sour thoughts as the cab rolled into the comparative brilliance of Lupin Square. In the muddle of increased traffic and bobbing heads of scuffling Chinks milling the sidewalks, I'd caught sight of a familiar thick-set figure.

It was Murdock. Head sunk between thick shoulders, stalking legs churning methodically, he drove a dogged course forward. There was no sign of his shadow, Delevan. The yellow men were falling back from that hard glance, eyeing him with sullen curious suspicion.

I'd just thumbed down my driver and dropped from the running board when the Chief disappeared into the head of Lam Kee alley. It was hard to believe my eyes. Dumb, that was it, chasing single-handed into the very spot where, six months since, he'd led a roaring riot squad on the tail of Hong Kong Fen, Poppy King.

TRUE, Fen was behind bars now, and his racket was scattered, but Chinks have a long memory, and above all, are opportunitists. Maybe, as Gorky had said, Murdock was following a hot tip on the Torquin knockover. It was as good a guess that seizing the chance as a lure, Fen men had planted a neat ambush for the officer.

The Chief's advent into the alley had drawn the Orientals like buzzing flies about the dark entrance. I shouldered swiftly through, set for trouble, right fist sweating my gat, handy in a side pocket. Murdock had already disappeared.

I brought up, scowling into the channeling dark.

There was movement in the black doorway at my elbow. I pivoted, flattening against the wall.

A voice said, "The Skipper just made Joy Lo's, Brandt."

It was Delevan, Murdock's shadow. I got the flash of his pale hatchet-like face under a wilted hat brim that partly hid his grim eyes.

"Check," I said, and shouldered off. He melted into the shadows again.

Fifty yards along, I made the entrance of Joy Lo's suey parlor. The Chief's advent had awakened interest and I elbowed through a cluster of curious loafers.

Tromping down four worn steps, I swung back the latticed doors. There was a long battered bar with fly-specked glass, a sawdust floor, a dozen tables surrounded by half drunken Chinks with a Fan-Tan layout drawing the most interest in the rear.

The dump was low-ceilinged, ill-lit. It smelled of cheap booze and sweaty bodies. At that it was a Sunday school compared to the dives in behind. Lo had a bad rep, was a short hop ahead of Atlanta in the dope racket.

He was nowhere in sight at first. Neither was Murdock.

I walked steps toward the bar. It brought to view a closed back door and the pot bellied body of Joy Lo stooped before the key hole. His elbows moved methodically as he wiped hands on a dirty apron.

At my elbow a barkeep said, "Yes?" and I said, "No."

I shoved back along the bar. Sawdust muted my steps as did the singsong of the lads at the Fan Tan spread.

Lo's arms ceased movement. I paused so close I could hear his hissing breath. I spoke his name softly, not oblivious of the quieting room about. The Chinks were interested in my play.

Lo choked once in his fat throat, spun round, hand flashing beneath his apron. A knife bulged there. I shook my head, grinning.

His ugly square face was a splotchy yellow. He made noises in his throat.

THE crowd laughed. He darted a venomous glance over my shoulder. It returned to my face. Then the mask spread. That's the Chink of it.

He hissed a "Well?" lips hardening.

"Murdock," I said. "Where is he?"

He spread moist palms.

I moved in, seizing a sweaty shirt front just under his racing Adam's apple.

"Save poker for punks," I gritted "Come on! Spill!"

Only the eyes changed, expressing glittering hate.

"Him there," he mumbled, jerking a thumb toward the panels.

"Yeaha? Who's with him?"

He slowly shook his head. "Him clome in—go back—thass all," he nodded glumly.

"Okay," I said, "but get this. There're bulls out front. It'd be too bad if anybody started anything. Sit tight and you're jake, Joy Lo, otherwise—"

I shoved him free. His fat shoulders slapped the wall and he stood staring buddha-like.

I turned the knob and pushed through into the back corridor. It was foul and dark. Whipping out my gat I made progress back. Maybe the bluff I'd slung into Lo's teeth would hold, maybe not. Whatever the Chief's business here, I was suggesting a quick scram, once I found him, to be on the safe side.

Doors ranked the wall. Most of 'em were closed but I knew what was back of them. Bunks for pipe-hitters. I paused, listening for sounds of talk. What I drew was deep snoring from somewhere and a weird high singsong chant. Some bozo was dreaming about peacock thrones. I smelled fuming opium.

A sweet spot it was for a Chief gone soft. God knows where Murdock was. I began opening doors. From the musty dark a hopped-up dame pulled a laugh and suggested entry. The snoring droned on, and the chanting.

Then three shots bellowed in quick succession. There came a choked cry. Almost before it died I'd raced to the hall's end, was trying the door there. It was locked. There was sound of hurried movement inside, the squeal of an opening window.

I threw a shoulder against the panels. At the third try the door burst in.

I brought up, staring.

The place was ten by ten, lit by a single-shaded mazda that haloed the baized top of a round card table. There were chairs around, cards and poker chips strewing the floor. At first I made out no occupant. My eyes lifted to the darkness of an opened window, jerked back.

Something stirred on the dark floor beyond the table. There was a deep groan. Kicking back a chair I lunged over.

Murdock sprawled the dirty boards there, limbs twitching feebly. I dropped to my knees, tugging at the limp shoulder.

"Chief," I gritted. "What the hell —who plugged you?"

He gasped, making gurgling noises in his throat. The once florid face was plaster white under the tossing mane of vital white hair. His eyes were closed. A ghastly wound in his chest welled red.

I shook him gently. "It's Lennox, Chief. Can't you speak?"

My ears were strained for the racing feet of Joy Lo's men from up front. There was nothing but thick silence. That and the chanting.

Murdock's lips began to move. I laid an ear close. He mumbled, "He — promised — information — on Torquin job." There was a pause. Red-flecked foam began to appear at the laxing lips. I knew what was to follow, the death rattle.

"Quick, Chief," I urged. "Can't you tell me who got you? Who—"

Stiffening lips twitched, mumbling brokenly. "Convert — Mission —" then dribbled off in the broken sentence. "He—said—I promised hop—didn't bring any—he shot—" The faintly moving lips stilled.

"Who—for God's sake, who?"

Gurgling rose deep in his throat. The shaggy head lolled sidewise.

CHIEF MURDOCK was dead. Sapped by some hop-head who'd thought to barter some information for snow. A dinky little snow-bird from a flop house Mission. Savagely, my eyes lifted, raking the room shadows.

Murdock's hat had rolled free in his fall. Another lay in a corner under, the open window. Rising, I leaped across, fishing it up.

It was a swanky gray snap brim with gilt initials stamping the sweat band, "B. S."

I grunted, eyes lifting to the dark window. It had been scant minutes since the killer had gone. I poked out a cautious head. Thick smelly blackness there. At the alley head toward the brightness of Lupin Square, a beat bull lumbered past. There was just the chance the murderer still lingered.

I threw a leg over the sill, dropped to the ground outside.

I was still in a crouch when a man hit my shoulders. The sudden attack socked me to the ground, but I lit, squirming, whipping back an elbow into a lean belly as circling arms vised my middle.

A grunt of pain laxed the hold, and rolling over, I drove up with both feet as a second figure from the dark rushed in. Chinks, these. I knew it from the method of attack and smell. My first attacker loomed over me, driving downward viciously. I threw sidewise and his steel bit the dirt, then I'd rolled to my feet as both men rushed in, gritting hot curses in Cantonese.

It was too dark to see, but that went for all of us. I dropped flat again, sensing that rush, and their bodies smacked together above me, wild arms thrashing. One of 'em got a nice shiv slash for he dropped back, choking.

I fired from the hip, dropping the second to his knees, and rocked upward in a swift rush that smacked the first man off balance, sending him crashing into the wall.

I left it at that. Through the window in that room of death I made out a tumbling flock of Orientals crowding in, led by the fat Joy Lo brandishing a knife.

Whether they were accessories to Murdock's kill, I couldn't tell, and right then it didn't matter. I was one against the mob and didn't care for the odds. I turned, racing for the lights of Lupin Square. When I got there I found I was still clutching the mussed up snap brim in my left hand.

I thumbed down a scab cab at the curb and tumbled in, the yellow pack on my heels. The driver tossed one startled look over his shoulder, jammed in his gears and leaped free of the curb as Lo's men spewed, fan-shaped, over the sidewalk.

Twenty minutes later we were parking in front of Headquarters.

CHAPTER II

Westward Bound

GHOSTS rode the room. Shadows of squirming crooks under fire, brazen molls and thick jowelled big shots who had long since answered the last call. There were other phantoms, too. Men in blue with big hands and hard, seamed faces, sharp-faced dicks, rookies—all memories now.

That dingy room with its big scarred desk, worn floor and smoke grimed ceiling, had been Murdock's bailiwick at Center City Headquarters for twenty years.

Just now a shaded mazda made mellow the desk top. Murdock's desk. But he was through with all that now. Three nights had passed since he'd bowed to the hot lead of a jittery red hot in Lam alley. A hop-head with the initials B. S. Blondie Spade they spelled when checked with the digit marks smearing that back room window. Another late development was the growing conviction that this

Spade was number three red-hot who had eluded the bulls in the Torquin mix. A timid eye witness had finally come forward with the description of the fleeing robber who had been the driver of the getaway car. He'd worn a mask but sported tow-colored hair, trim waxed mustache and gray snap brim. Several perfumed cigarette butts had been found at the spot in the alley where the car had stood before the knockover. "Hamuds." Blondie was known to affect this brand.

Just why Blondie had contacted the Chief afterward was the riddle. Skeptics grinned when they told of Blondie's conversation at the Lupin Square Mission. Nevertheless I agreed with Gorky in surmising that fact had much to do with the officer and red-hots getting together at Joy Lo's dump. Maybe the little hop-head had got cold feet. Maybe his conscience hurt him.

Rather, I'd guess he was pulling a fast one by offering to squawk for a bunch of hot snow before he scrammed. Dream stuff was hard to get, even at such places as Lo's, with the federals on a local rampage.

My hunch was that the Chief hadn't fallen for the plant, thirded too much knowledge out of Blondie and got killed for his pains.

THE hours following Murdock's death had been filled with desperate search. Grim-faced squads tromping inexorably the back courts and alleys, hideaways, and hop joints of the River district. But the results to date had been zero. Blondie Spade had vanished and with him a sweet bunch of loot. The search had scarcely slackened for the big funeral at Fairmont, one of the largest in Center City's history. Murdock had had many friends. Gorky and I had ridden back together from the cemetery.

Now, across that desk, as Acting Chief, he shuffled his feet and cleared his throat. The lean chiseled features were haggard and drawn but the wide shoulders were unrelenting. A muscle started working in his bronzed jaw. He said flatly through his teeth, "Murdock's wife had a stroke at the funeral this afternoon. She'll never walk again."

"Yeaha," I answered. "That's the hell of it. Lead from a lousy punk like Spade seldom stops travelling with one man down."

"And some come up," Gorky said, a hard smile twitching at his lips. "I'll be the next Chief, Brandt, due to Murdock's going, but by God," his fist crashed the desk top, "I'd rip every stripe off my sleeve if he could be sitting in this chair right now! I'm hounding Blondie Spade to hell before I call it a day."

I said, "It begins to look a tough nut to crack, as an eye-opener, Gorky."

He poked a finger, clipping, "Correct! The minute that mole-faced little gorilla put the smear on Murdock, he changed addresses. You know the fight we've made. There isn't a rookie on the force that hasn't made it a personal thing." He shrugged helpless shoulders. "This Blondie's a memory right now."

I grunted, fishing for a pill.

"What's more," Gorky bored on, "I've wired the big burgs, broadcasted descriptions and plastered Spade's mug at every crossroad—what's the result?" He spread his palms. "I think you understand my position, Brandt. Murdock had his enemies on the City Council. You know human nature. They're squawking now that if Murdock had had the guts a chief should have, he wouldn't have got plugged." He jumped to his feet, stalked to the door, swung round. "My hands are tied, Lennox. If I sent special dicks all over the country tailing down clues on city cash—"

"They'd be on *your* neck," I finished.

"Right. Well, to hell with 'em as far as that goes, but opposition is keen, and there're three members I might mention who are teetering in a general shakeup of the force. That means a lot of good men would lose their jobs if I give provocation. I've got to play things close to my vest, savvy?"

"So what?" I asked.

"So this!" He barged across, leaned over the desk. "The boys have authorized me to send you to K.C." He straightened, slapping a check book on the scarred mahogany.

I stared a moment, swallowed once and got to my feet. "Gorky," I said, "will you put that damn thing away before I get sore? How many times do you suppose Murdock forgot his prejudices and yanked me out of the red? He was a grand guy and a good copper. Would I get a personal kick out of slapping the screws on his killer? I've made some jack in my time and the lads can keep their dough. If you ask me, I pulled a sweet muff in ever letting the Chief out of my sight over in Lupin Square. If you guess Spade has fanned for Kansas City, it's me for the River town."

Gorky's hand flashed out. I gripped it.

He said, "By God, you're not surprising me, Brandt." He held my eyes a moment, then resumed his seat.

"Here's the dope," he offered.

Maybe Blondie Spade took a train, maybe he travelled west by motor. I hooked a United Air Luxury Liner and by midnight with a Gladstone and shoulder gat for company, I'd shaken the dust of two states off my wings.

Boring along through the bumpy night, my thoughts kept time to the revving motors up front. For once the bulls were at my back. As a usual thing, I played a lone wolf rôle, asked no aid nor quarter, blazed my own pathways. I knew the night. Perhaps there were faster men with a rod, but the proof of the pudding is the eating, and I was still taking my groceries.

The Human Flash. That was my billing in old vaudeville days. The news hawks were still calling me that. I suppose they referred to my draw. Okay. Well, it was going to take it all on the cold trail of this killer.

I stared out into the rushing dark. Far below the lights of a town twinkled cozily. The Indiana ceiling was getting rough and rain began to beat against the panes. There was a light passenger list; most of the folks had turned in, but I didn't feel that way.

I fished out the "mugg" and jotted notations Gorky had given me, and sat studying them under the dim light.

SPADE was a two time loser, five feet seven, weight one thirty-five. He had tow-colored hair and pale narrow eyes running to a squint. He affected a small mustache, waxed at the tips and perfumed cigarettes. There was a mole on the left side of his chin.

He was a flashy dresser and haunted the burlesque shows. That last spelled dames to Gorky in capital letters. He'd run three or four jazzy wrens to earth the past two days who had mamma'd Blondie at odd moments but they all swore Spade was in last year's almanac. They hadn't seen him in weeks.

The long shot tip that was sending me to the Missouri metroplis was a torn up telegram Gorky had sleuthed out of the wastebasket at Spade's rooms. Pieced together it revealed a late K.C. date and read:

PIERCE STUFF THE NUTS STOP ANSWERS ARE STILL SOFT STOP BE SEEING YOU
C L

Greek at first, sure, but coupled with a girl's photo on the dresser signed Connie Lusk, it was the pretzels. For one of the burlesque wrens identified Connie as Blondie's number one sweetie "out west somewhere" and wired dope from Flannery, K. C. chief, proved Blondie Spade a local product who hadn't been round in some time. As for Connie Lusk, Flannery reported her home talent, also, a cabaret singer, with a smelly rep who had been star witness in a late blackmail case out there.

Her testimony had pretty well cleared the skirts of a shyster attorney named Grant Pierce. It was reported the two were engaged to be married soon. In the light of this dope, Gorky insisted Blondie had likely got jealous of Pierce and Connie had wired to reassure him. The "be seeing you" suggested a rendezvous. Whether that meeting was to be in K. C. or somewhere else, whether Blondie would keep the engagement after ironing out Murdock, was the chance we had to take.

Dawn was smearing the east as the big tri-motor went into a roaring circle above the crazy-quilt patchwork of city streets below, dropped swiftly from smoky low hanging clouds and skimmed the drowsy gray expanse of the big river. It was five a.m. as we tractioned to a swift halt in the long sandy runways fronting the Airways station.

CHAPTER III

Threads of Vengeance

I HOOKED a few hours sleep at the Mulbach, ate, showered, and contacted Flannery at H.Q.

I spent an hour with him. It didn't rate me so much. The Chief didn't think Blondie was around as yet, at least, hadn't been spotted, though they'd kept eyes out for him. The Lusk woman had been seen with the shyster Pierce in his car the previous evening. He didn't think it would be tough contacting her, once we started. His suspicion that Pierce was a big time fence, among other things, about summed up the story.

I did tall thinking over two cold beers in the hotel bar and decided to brace the lawyer.

If he, like Spade, was sweet on Connie, he might welcome the chance to point a hot finger in the hophead's direction. I could hover Connie later. On second thought, I phoned the chief. I figured a word from him would rate me an interview with the lawyer, and it did.

After half an hour, I dialed Pierce and he said he would see me, after lunch. He wasn't far over, in the Mandan Building on Fourteenth. A cage got me to the tenth level and I found his stand. Black letters on a glass door said:

P. GRANT PIERCE
Attorney at Law

Inside was a small waiting room, with a railing. Clattering typewriter keys paused abruptly as I stepped forward. The thin girl, in a linen suit behind the desk, fumbled at a stringy bob and pulled a smile. It didn't help her face much. Her teeth were crooked and her mouth was too wide. Her pale eyes under mascaraed lashes held that haunted, disappointed look common to sex-hungry maiden ladies. She chewed gum.

She flushed as my glance swept down over her stream-lining and snapped curtly:

"Well?"

I lifted brows, nodding the door marked private. "Mr. Pierce," I said.

"He's engaged right now," she munched. "Eating his lunch."

"Thanks," I said. "He'll see me." I swung the gate and strode forward.

"Not now—not now—" she chirped, rising hurriedly.

"Relax, Sis," I tossed over a shoulder. "This is important." I seized the knob and passed through the door into the inner office.

Pierce wasn't in sight. There was the usual desk, littered with papers, chairs, filing cabinets flanking a small closet door.

The odd note in the set-up was a tall shelving plant stand crammed to the gunwales with a dozen different varieties of cacti. The commoner brands were planted in long dirt-filled troughs, but swanky specimens, some of which were blooming, were potted singly.

There was a small table fronting the stand that carried a roll of brown wrapping paper, pen, ink, a scrawled address on a mailing sticker. There was a ball of twine and an open shoe box that had been carefully packed with a dozen or so plants, ready for shipping.

The whole set-up suggested the enthusiastic amateur. It was a sidelight on the shyster's character.

Funny thing about men. I knew a big shot once who didn't turn a hair when a guy swiped his wife. He ironed out that same bozo for kicking one of his pet tom cats. I guessed Pierce thought a lot of his cacti.

For the rest, two windows showed out on the street and one, on the left, gave on a fire escape. A baize screen partially hid a medium-sized safe in the far corner. The street windows were closed, green shades lowered. Traffic noises drifted up through the fire escape window which stood sash high.

I crossed to the desk. The remains of a half eaten lunch was spread on a large tray. The attorney's chair was pushed back. His napkin was on the floor. A dictaphone motor, still rotating, was shoved to one side. The mouthpiece dangled, clucking sounds as the record spun.

The attorney couldn't be far. I got over to the open window, lit a pill.

Across the twelve-foot alley well a workman was busy on the roof, patching a broken chimney. Heat rose from the tar in waves. He finished, swabbing his face. I guessed it was hot as hell out there. He picked up his extension ladder. Enough of that.

I swung round, thinking Pierce must be a busy man dictating even during meals. I crossed over and sat down in Pierce's chair. It was the swivel type, comfortable looking. I turned on the small desk fan at my elbow. It churned life into the hot air. I yawned, glancing at my watch.

The typing had ceased in the outer office. A door slammed. I guessed the blonde had gone for food. Or maybe it was Pierce coming back. I wondered idly how he'd passed the girl without her knowing it.

The dictaphone clicked on. I cut the switch. Kind of funny about Pierce. He'd named the hour. One p.m. It was a quarter after that now. Guessing police business, he'd be prompt.

I stretched wearily. Not so much sleep the past twenty-four hours.

THEN, without warning, something struck like a pile driver. An ear splitting explosion that rocked the casements and sent me head first to the floor. Numbing pain vised my skull, raced down my spine. I forgot things, as star-smeared dark swallowed consciousness.

I came to, nose against the mop board, stared round dazedly and rocked unsteadily to my feet. The place had been neatly bombed and showed a mess. The green screen sprawled the floor in a litter of papers and documents. The shattered safe door yawned wide and two of the drawers had spewed out their contents. Every wall picture had fallen, adding to the litter. Hot wind gusted in through the shattered pane of the street window. The curtain snapped monotonously. I grunted, sopping at a bruised head with a pocket handkerchief.

It was a sweet set-up I'd walked into. What the devil was its meaning? For the moment it looked like some sort of plant Pierce had set for me. It was a cinch he hadn't been minutes gone when I blew in. Still, the idea didn't make sense. The shyster couldn't even guess my mission. Flannery would have been damn laconic about that. It looked more like I'd taken the jolt meant for the lawyer—some malcontent blasting *him* out.

I scowled toward the door. The lad sure was conspicuous by his absence. I listened for interruption from the people in the other offices about. None came. I recalled that even the stenographer was out. What the devil did it all mean?

I turned slowly, eyes raking the place, glance settling on the closed closet door. Then I saw the blood!

It was forming slowly in a pool at the sill. Springing forward, I seized the knob and jerked the door open. A man came tumbling out into my arms. I lowered him to the floor, guessing it was Pierce. He had been stabbed twice in the throat.

I grunted, glancing at the closet. A shallow affair used for papers and manuscripts. Pierce had been knifed, then propped, standing in the closet by the closed door. He was thin-framed, small-featured, with a beak of a nose. He wore glasses, still in place. His near-bald head carried a fringe of reddish hair. Brows and lashes matched it. He was in his shirt sleeves and wore well pressed blue trousers and vest. There were blood spots on his shiny oxfords. He wore clock-worked silk socks.

I straightened, studying him. Some things were becoming rather evident. Whoever had blown that safe had first killed the lawyer, placed him in the closet, then set the bomb fuse. All this before I'd entered the room. The blonde? Hardly. Women of her type don't sit calmly chewing gum and waiting for safes to explode.

There was but one deduction left. The guy that had been in that office just before me was after something in Pierce's safe. I was the innocent mystander who had blundered in just in time to take the sock. But what the devil had become of him?

I walked to the window, poked out a head, scanning the fire escape. A dead cigarette butt adhered to one of the cross rails.

That hadn't been there when I first entered the room. I was used to noticing such things. So the illusive safe cracker had entered while I lay blotto in the corner. Mounting the sill, I retrieved the cigarette butt. It was a cork tip and there was scorched gilt lettering still showing "Hamud." I smelled of it. Perfumed.

I pocketed it grimly. Across four states a certain pale-faced red-hot had been known to use such fags. It wasn't a coincidence I'd found it here.

I ran narrowed eyes over the rusty railing. There were unmistakable scratches there. The escape angled off down the building's side. I thought of the workmen on the roof across the way. The guy with the ladder. He'd disappeared.

I swung back into the room. It was a mix for the cops, all right, but first I was taking a good look. I rated it, considering the sock I'd taken a few minutes since.

I lit a fresh pill, staring down at the dead man, thoughts suddenly reverting to Connie Lusk. Funny, dames fell for such men, or had she? I was guessing Blondie Spade more her weak moment. She'd wired Blondie "Pierce stuff the nuts." But maybe Blondie questioned that. What of the cigarette butt on the landing? Maybe the boys had had words.

I crossed to the safe.

From the looks of the shattered lock and the clutter about, someone unused to nitro had pulled that job. A real box man would have used less soup. I crouched, scanning the heap of papers. Letters, abstracts of title, deeds. All useless as far as I was concerned. Then I made a find.

On the floor of one of the sprung safe drawers lay an oblong bit of paper, not larger than a finger. It was a sticker such as jewelry firms use on small packing boxes. Tiny black letters leaped at me. They spelled a swell story: "Torquin's." The Center City loot had lain in that drawer!

I raced furiously through the remaining compartments, most of which showed unmistakable marks of jimmying. I found nothing but more tracts and knick-knacks. The gems were gone!

I straightened. The lawyer's coat hung on a hall tree in the opposite corner. I crossed and fanned the pockets, exposing a small loose leaf notebook. There were jotted memoranda there, meaningless figures. I leafed it through. On the back page in the lawyer's characteristic scrawl appeared a list of names, all feminine:

Dolly—Ardmore 2-379
Anne French—Stockdale 4-446
Belle, Bessie— . . .

A long list. Some were crossed. My glance ran down, settling on the last entry.

"Connie Lusk." The telephone number was scratched. I frowned. It was just one of those things.

The phone rang! Shoving the book in a side pocket, I crossed to the desk and stood glaring at it. It rang again. I picked up the instrument.

"Yes?" I lipped.

"Hello, Piercy," a feminine voice said. "Where did you get to last night? You-all haven't forgotten little Connie, have you?"

I swallowed. The soft southern tones were music over the wire. My fingers tensed on the receiver. The thought flashed, "The Lusk girl! Now I've got it, what'll I do with it?"

"No, baby," I bluffed, speaking low. "Be natural, will you?"

There came a moment's strained silence, then, "Your voice sounds funny, sugar. Well, I just called to say Hooly's stuck me on for another turn at twelve, damn 'im, but I'll be seein' you tonight in our booth after that, and don't stand me up again, I don't swallow that so well. As for the password on the dream stuff you can tell your friends it's *Cyprus* tonight. That'll rate 'em a few decks. 'Bye."

"'Bye," I mumbled, and hung up. Dream stuff with a password. Decks—that spelled dope shoving. So, among other things Connie was messing round in a hop joint. My glance dropped to the dead man on the floor. No, Piercy wouldn't be buying drinks for any dame in Hooly's around midnight, wherever that was, but there was a chance I might fill his spot.

I picked up the instrument, called headquarters, asking for Flannery.

"Hello, Chief," I said. "Brandt Lennox speaking. Well, I busted up for an interview with Lawyer Pierce after calling you, and tie this—I found him croaked. Stabbed twice in the neck and propped up in his office closet. Some bozo set a time apple on the safe and I got here just in time to get a K.O. myself. What? Nope, not a sign of 'im. I'm guessing he lammed down the fire escape. Me? I'm all right. I'll stick here till you send somebody. I'll give the dope to the boys. Okay."

A door slammed in the outer office. I decided to go out. The fading Garbo was parking her hat on a hook. She glanced around.

"Oh, you," she said.

"Yeah." I tilted my hat down over my bruised brow. She came through the wicket gate, flounced down in her chair and ruffled her stringy bob. Her thin legs showed through the stuff of her skirt. I wondered at Pierce's judgment.

I crossed, sat on the edge of her desk and asked, "Been a lot of folks here this morning?"

She drew down her brows. "A few," she answered. She sensed my temp' hadn't risen any at sight of her. The thought didn't improve her temper any.

"Who, for instance?"

She shrugged thin shoulders. "Who wants to know?"

I tossed down a card. She picked it up, staring.

"A detective—oh!"

"Yeah." I held her startled glance, gave it to her straight. "Somebody's croaked the boss in there. Now get your answers ready."

"Killed?" she choked, face going as white as paper. "But I don't understand. Mr. Pierce killed?"

Her hands fluttered futilely at her throat. She rose, sagging there a moment. She got one long look, then slumped to the floor in a faint.

I crossed to the cooler, drew off a cupful of water and, walking back to the girl, dashed it in her face. She gasped twice, then came to, sputtering, pawing at her skirt that had jerked high, exposing laced undies and a well defined run in her gartered sock. I helped her up and over to a chair. She slumped there, crying dolefully. I waited a moment, then said, "Tough stuff, sister, but every minute we waste, the killer's dusting his heels. Try to think now. Who was the last person in this office ahead of me?"

"Why — why, Kerrigan, Hooly Kerrigan."

"And just who is Kerrigan?"

"The—the boss of—the Cypress Bell, a—a river boat club," she stammered.

"So," I says. "When was that?"

"Around noon."

"The two men seem to be having any trouble about anything?"

"Yes, they were quarrelling. I could

hear Kerrigan swearing terribly through the door."

"Could you understand what it was all about?"

"Kerrigan mentioned decks—I suppose he was referring to his boat and —and Mr. Pierce spoke something about not worrying over the late snow. That seemed funny, it was so hot." She frowned, swallowing noisily, then added, "Too, there was a woman, a singer at the club."

"Connie Lusk?"

Her glance jerked up. "Why—why, yes. How did you know?"

"Never mind that. Hear anything else?"

"Yes. Kerrigan — he — he threatened to kill somebody, I—I suppose it was Mr. Pierce." The sentence was scarcely a whisper.

My eyes went thoughtful on that one. Here was a third party to the murder picture that had so far showed Pierce and a guy that smoked Hamud cigarettes, the elusive Blondie Spade. Maybe I was previous. There seemed to be a lot of birds steamed up over the chorine, Connie. I frowned, thinking about her phone message, the words about dream stuff. Then I thought of the jewelry sticker and asked:

"This Kerrigan, what does he smoke?"

"Smoke?" she rammed knuckles in her mouth.

"Yeah!" I snapped. "Cigars or cigarettes?"

"Why—why he was smoking a cigar when—"

"Okay," I said. "And there wasn't anybody else in the room here after Kerrigan left? When was that?"

"About twelve-fifteen. No. Mr. Pierce called me in to give me some briefs. I came out and he began using the dictaphone."

"How long did that last?"

"Half an hour maybe. Then he asked me to order his lunch from the restaurant downstairs."

"When was the last noise you heard from in there?"

Her penciled brows puckered in thought.

"Maybe twenty minutes before you came in."

"You didn't hear any outcry? Anything to indicate Pierce had been attacked?"

"No—no. Nothing at all." She began crying again. Spoke with difficulty. "The — dictating — just stopped."

I turned toward the door. Heavy feet were scuffing in the hall. The outer door opened, showing three cops and a fourth man in plain clothes. They came in.

"Logan," lipped the detective from headquarters, slouching forward and extending a hand. "You're Lennox, I s'pose. What's the dope here?" He was tall and thin, with a slouch. The eyes were sleepy, but had a habit of suddenly narrowing, going bright. He wore wrinkled blue serge and built his own cigarettes. One dangled now from his lower lip.

I explained the situation briefly, named my hotel and left. The girl still crouched low in her chair, eyes on space. I guessed maybe Pierce had been good to her at times. I felt sorry for her.

CHAPTER IV

The Cypress Queen

I WENT down worn cellar steps and blundered round in the dark until I heard sounds of pounding. I was in the basement of the Organ Building across the alley from the Mandan block and was hunting Harlin, the janitor. The pounding led me to the big old-fashioned fire box. He shoved a head round the corner, squinting at me.

"What the hell do you want?" he growled suspiciously. "If you're the insurance inspector I'll have this old hearse-heater okay maybe before snow flies."

"Wait," I grinned, offering a fat cigar. "I'm just a dick out working on the Pierce case."

His sooty face relaxed and he stepped out, tossing aside a big wrench and swabbing black palms on his faded overalls. He was a big lad with a nice grin, once he trusted you.

"The law, huh?" he grunted, accepting the smoke. "Pierce case? I don't get you."

We parked on the coal box. "Lawyer Pierce got killed over in the Mandan Building round noon today," I informed him while he lit up. "We're fanning the premises."

"That shyster? I always said some one'd get his number—" He broke off, puffing prodigiously.

"His rep wasn't so sweet at that," I said. "But murder's murder." I gestured the furnace. "Been patching her up some, I see."

"Yep. Cellar to roof. She's an old plant. City inspectors been ridin' our tails."

I nodded, eyes running over his burly frame.

"You weren't on the roof, say round twelve today, fixing the main chimney?"

"Nope, had a helper up there on that, a damn hitch hiker that's been pesterin' me for work the last day or so."

"So? Well, Pierce's office window overlooks your roof here. Maybe this bozo saw something. Is he round somewhere?"

"Nope. Drew his time and left half an hour ago."

I grunted, spoke casually. "Sort of a big guy, stoop shouldered, dark?"

"Him?" he waved the fuming stogie. "Hell, no. A white-faced, smooth shaven little runt that could hardly tote a ladder."

I tensed forward. "Swell," I offered, "and a mole on his chin."

HE frowned, spitting. Then shook a shaggy head. "No mole," he decided at length. "Had adhesive over a chin boil he said was botherin' some—"

I got up. "Well, that's that," I said. "Thanks for the time."

"That's all right," he grinned, rising. "Always glad to help the law, specially when they fetch seegars."

"Check." I made for the stairs.

I'd established one thing. Small doubt the scab mason had been Blondie Spade, *sans* mustache, with adhesive over the tell-tale mole. The thing added well. Posing as a workman, he'd slid across the alley well on the extension ladder and sapped the lawyer. Guessing a locked safe, he'd toted a small time bomb to crack the crib.

It had been sheer happenstance I'd blundered into the plant while he was out on the roof waiting for the thing to explode. Presence of the jewelry sticker in the safe drawer argued Blondie had passed the Torquin loot to Pierce probably for fencing.

The rest was a mystery. Whether the lawyer had tried some double cross for the gems, or whether the stabbing had been a crime of passion, considering the Connie Lusk angle, the result was the same. Blondie had repossessed the loot and scrammed. I'd been short minutes from a sweet collar in that visit to the office. It didn't make me feel any better.

There was one lead left. The girl. Even she was a quantity X. Maybe, learning of the killing, she'd fade from the picture, too. But I guessed not. From all I'd heard of her, she was a pretty wise sister. Would play things carefully, realizing her association with Pierce was common knowledge and a scram would point a guilty finger.

I had a few hours to kill. I decided on the Regent. They ran a double bill and the hot streets were showing shadows when I left the Marquee, already glittering with colored electrics. I got to thinking about the comedy picture, run between features, as I tromped down Main Street, headed for the hotel and supper. "Easy Pickens" had been the title. Pickens was the name of the copper who'd made a pinch. Riding along in the patrol wagon toward the station, the rat faced poke lifter had slipped his loot, some jazzy gems hooked off a swell dame in a department store, into the bull's pocket, and the clever little devil just missed walking out a free man when the trick was discovered. It had pulled a lot of laughs but there was four square truth in the gag.

More than one bull has muffed a pinch by searching strange fields when the jack pot lies hidden in his own front yard.

MY cab jounced down the levee ramp and slewed in toward the curb. I got out, fishing for change, eyes running over the lay below.

Kerrigan's *Cypress Queen* lay moored at the foot of Dock Street. Taxies were milling round and customers were tromping up and down the gang plank. I could make out plenty of people beyond on the glittering decks. Music wafted up. Through wide-slung windows I glimpsed a crowded dining saloon and couples rocking round on the dance floor.

I paid off and approached a hard-faced flunkie in a uniform coat and yachting britches handing folks up the 'plank. His hard glance raked me and he thumbed me up and over. I made the deck, the main door entrance. Some dump.

A bunch of shades were blaring blues in the pit fronting the drop curtain at the upper end. Dusty potted palms were parked around. Jap lanterns shaded the drop lights. Latticed booths edged the waxed floor. There were some tables fronting them. The jostling, laughing, yelling crowd was lit to a man. I got the smell of food, hootch, stale tobacco and sweat. It was hot. I grabbed off a table in an open-work booth and sat down. A thin waiter in a soiled apron slid up and lifted an agile eyebrow. Working on a hunch, I thumbed him closer. He stooped, eyeing me narrowly.

I lurched toward him, hiccoughing. "Cyprus," I husked, displaying three fingers.

I heard breath hiss through his teeth. His face went mask-like. He pulled a startled grunt.

I nodded solemnly, drunkenly holding his eyes. "I might mention 'nother name, jus' in case," I whispered, dropping a slow wink. "It's Pierce. Tha' mean anything to you?"

His face cleared a little.

"Okay," he muttered, and heeled off down the booth row.

I'd really intended keeping the dream stuff and the "Cypress" tip as an ace in the hole. But my glance had dropped to the hands of my wrist watch. They'd said five till twelve. If I intended sitting in on any kind of game on the *Cypress Queen*, it was high time I started. My glance ran over the place again. There were several come-on dames working the stags and I got to wondering which one was Connie.

A TOUCH on my elbow swung me round. It was my waiter. He slapped a napkin down and some silverware. His back pretty well filled the latticed opening. He stooped, arranging the spoons, and lipped from the side of his mouth.

"Fifty bucks."

"Ouch," I said too loud, and he frowned.

My eyes dropped to the napkin. The corner of a white envelope showed there. I nodded, fumbling for my roll. Peeling off two twenties and a ten, I wadded them up and shoved them into his cupped palm, resting on the table edge.

He said, "Yes, sir," and turned away.

I grabbed the corner of his apron. "Jus' a minute," I offered. "Thish Lusk dame, Connie Lusk. When's she come on?" I thumbed the stage.

He frowned down out of his masklike face. Sweat glistened on his upper lip.

"Jus' another boy frien'," I grinned. "Like to see her." I tossed a dollar to the table top.

"Yes, sir, why pretty soon now, sir, midnight." He nodded the stage.

"Anything you could do, you unnerstan'?" I spread palms.

A smile cracked his frozen face. The eyes stayed hard. "Sure," he said, and scuffed off.

I fingered the envelope in my coat pocket. I didn't know how I was going to use it just yet but I held a sweet club over that joint.

The house went dim just then and the footlights leaped to life. I swung, facing the stage as the curtain rose. A half dozen chorines in scanties tromped on to a tinkle of jazz that melted into a southern lullaby. They were followed by a hot little mama that brought the crowd to its feet in a roar of applause. Small doubt she was Connie Lusk.

The girls dropped upstage, vamping, and Connie stepped to the foot trough. She wore a glittering black evening gown, low in the neck. Chiffon panels swung from her waist, drifting about her as she moved, slowly, seductively, to the crooning wail of the muted orchestra. Her crooning notes were rich, low and compelling. The kind that pried into a man's vitals.

Don' know where youse gone, hon,
Spec's it's far away,
All I know I's mournin'
For you night and day.

Her arms and shoulders gleamed ivory white in the soft light. The lids of her wide-spaced, heavily mascaraed eyes closed. Her smooth shoulders swayed, sensitive features worked with emotion. I heard a rustling about me. The crowd was swaying in unison.

Suddenly she paused, stiffened. Her eyes flew wide. Fists clenched. The wail rose to a throaty shout:

But does you fool me, Honey,
Does you prove untrue,
I'll scratch yo' lovin' eyes out,
I'll mark yo' black and blue.

The music paused on a blue crash of chords and cymbals. Connie bowed to the boards. The crowd yelled and stomped. Flowers showered the stage. Three times she repeated the number. Then the curtain fell. Connie stepped out and came down short steps to the floor of the restaurant, began mixing among the guests. I watched her, narrow-eyed, as she drifted to the room's far end.

A man appeared at my elbow. I glanced up. He was dressed in a baggy tuxedo and wore a carnation in his button-hole. His face was bland and running to fat rolls at the low collar. He wore a black toupee and a short bristly mustache. He beamed down through gold-rimmed nose glasses. He held a menu card in his pudgy right fist.

I studied him keenly, without appearing to do so. I was guessing this was Hooly Kerrigan, the boss. The man who had quarrelled with Grant Pierce an hour before his death.

"Find everything all right, sir?" he beamed.

"I'sh schwell," I grinned. "Perfec'ly schwell."

"I understand you were asking for Miss Lusk. She wasn't going on tonight, but there were so many requests—" He shrugged thick shoulders. "Well, when the public demands—"

"Real talent," I offered solemnly.

"Absolutely." He waved the card. I glanced round. Connie Lusk was at his elbow.

"Another admirer, Miss Lusk. He looks lonely too."

Connie flashed pearly teeth and slid into a chair. Kerrigan bowed and hurried away.

"Not treatin' you right, big boy?" she lisped.

"Can't complain," I muttered.

"Buy me a drink, hon?" she asked next. I could feel the great dark eyes studying my face.

"Okay," I grinned, pounding on the table.

My waiter appeared. A trifle too soon, I thought. I said, "Spirits for the lady, Joe."

"Not forgetting the gent," she laughed, picking up my glass and handing it to the man. He shuffled away.

I studied the girl. On close inspection there was a certain hardness to the languorous lips, a glint in the soft eyes. She looked better behind the footlights.

She leaned across as the orchestra muted into the "Memphis Blues." Her heavily beaded dress sagged at the V. I deliberately estimated her charms. She was expecting that.

She covered my hand with her own white one. My nerves thrilled to a warning. I was getting more attention than I'd bargained for. Why?

"Don't look so sour, dearie. Listen to that music. Don't it get into your feet?"

I grinned. "A trifle under the influence, sister, if you get me," I explained.

"That's okay. Drowndin' your troubles, eh? Let's dance."

I reeled up. The girl rose, rounded the small table, lifted her arms, nestling against me. I was conscious of her soft body, the lure of her. We moved out onto the floor. She snuggled her dark head against my neck and sighed. Her hair tickled my nose. She used musk perfume. She had appeal, no denying that. She glanced up, smiled. I said:

"Nize baby. Kid should be on big time."

"Thanks, goodlookin'."

We finished the mill. I caught the question in her eyes as we reached our table again. The music died. We sat down. Drinks waited. She lifted her glass. "To you, handsome," she smiled.

We drank.

I was thinking fast. I'd have to get this dame outside somewhere, somehow, before I could put on the screws. She had too many friends around.

The waiter appeared, slapping down glasses. That was a bit raw. I hadn't even ordered. I decided the joint knew how to work its drunks.

"Don't forget your turn, Miss Lusk," he said, staring hard at the girl.

"Okay," she shrugged.

He turned away without a glance at me. I sipped at the hootch. It tasted bitter. Knockout drops. My nerves leaped. It was my first hunch I was sitting in on some plant.

A drunk was making a disturbance at the door. Two bouncers were working on him. Connie turned languidly. I slopped the contents of my glass in the spittoon at my feet, coughing noisily.

To the observer, here was only a hostess gold-bricking a half drunk sucker. But the sudden realization struck me that Kerrigan must have made me out for what I was. That Connie was playing come-on for the night club owner. She turned, smiling.

"It's cool out on deck. Let's stroll, eh, hon?"

THE action hid the light in my eyes. Here was a break. Maybe Connie figured she was nosing me into the tiger's mouth. Well, I'd cracked such jaws before and it might be an "out" with the girl.

She took my arm and we made for a door halfway down the room. We reached it and Connie seized the doorknob. We swung out into a low corridor.

Beneath a reeling exterior my nerves were taut as fiddle strings. I bumped the girl at every step, my right hand hovering near my coat lapel, inches from a draw. The corridor was narrow. Connie closed the door.

"To your right, big boy," she breathed. I noticed her bosom was rising and falling quickly. She was excited about something.

"Ladies firs', always," I said, and shoved her a bit roughly ahead of me. We went down the corridor, passing two doors. She paused.

"Here?" I asked.

"Uh-huh," she breathed. I turned the knob, shoved against the panel. I caught a glimpse of a small storeroom with stacked cartons and boxes. The place smelled stuffy. My glance swept the girl's face. Her pearly teeth were sunk in her under lip. Her black eyes were dilated and staring over my shoulder.

That wasn't all. There had been the noise of a softly closed door behind. My hand shot out, clamping her white wrist. I crowded her through, surged after her, slamming the door behind me. There came the thudding pound of feet outside. Muttered cursing. The room was dimly lighted by a single electric dangling from the ceiling. Still retaining the girl's wrist, I shot the bolt. The knob rattled futilely. Fists pounded on the door. There came sounds of angry voices.

I swung on Connie. She shrank back, terrified, widening eyes on my face, one hand covering her mouth.

The pounding continued on the panels at my back. I glared around. The room wasn't more than eight feet square, probably gave off on the kitchen from the looks of the piled stores that half-filled the space. There was another door. Leaping across, I bolted that. None too soon. The knob turned stealthily almost before I had finished.

It was a sweet plant. Kerrigan had lured me here to bump me off. My body was likely slated for the river. Dead dicks tell no tales.

Then I made out the trap in the floor. I palmed my gat, covering the cringing girl.

Sudden muffled firing broke out in the corridor. Lead began plucking ugly holes about the lock. I lunged back against Connie out of the line of fire. There was the monotonous muffled blare of loudly played jazz. I lipped grimly:

"Quiet, kid. I'll plug you sure as hell if you try any tricks." Stooping, I jerked up on the trap by the steel ring at my feet. A bullet clipped through, thudding the opposite wall. From below came the sound of lapping water. I stared down. The next instant, eyes grown accustomed to the gloom, I made out a small boat moored there.

Straightening, I seized the girl. The corridor door was splitting under stoutly applied shoulders. Time was short. My eyes swept down over the panelled gown. I shot out a hand, jerking the chiffon panels from her dress, whirled her round and bound her wrists with the flimsy stuff. It would serve for a moment and a moment was all I needed.

Connie crouched back against the wall, sobbing. She slid to the floor. Stooping, I bound her silken ankles with more chiffon. Then, lifting her bodily, I tumbled her into the bobbing boat, below. The next instant I'd followed. Without pausing to drop the trap, I fumbled in the darkness, found an oar. Casting off the loosely looped painter, I shoved off into the black current.

CHAPTER V

Double Double-Cross

CONNIE LUSK sat writhing in the chair. I'd clapped cuffs on her wrists through the rungs. We were in my room at the hotel. I'd caught a cab on lower Dock Street and hustled my unwilling charge back up town where we could talk.

She'd been a sweet handful there at first, but the cab driver had taken my word for it I was taking a bad sister home after a bust on the levee; this, after I'd softened his suspicion with a fiver.

Now she'd gone sullen. But from the twitching of her lips and the frantic look growing in her eyes I guessed my thirding was wearing her down. I stood watching her.

"Ready to talk, Connie?"

"I don't know anything." She swayed her head from side to side.

"Don't be a sap," I repeated for the dozenth time. "I've come across four states to grab Blondie Spade, and write this down, I'm taking him, see? Tell me where he is and you can do a single out that door."

Her head wagged monotonously.

"Come again, sister. Back at the Club you and that waiter and Kerrigan pulled a frame-up on me. Got suspicious as hell when I asked for you. Why?"

Still she did not answer.

"Where's Blondie?" I reached down, lifting her chin.

"How the hell should I know, you lousy dick!"

I shrugged. "I can grease things for you, sister."

"Yeah," she flashed up at me. "I've heard that line before. You're ridin' a goofy hunch hard, you sap. You think you're so wise. Well, listen.

You're dumb, hear me? Dumb as hell!" Her voice rose to a near shriek. "If you know so much, why don't you pull your pinch?" She laughed hysterically.

"So, you're stickin' to that, eh? Dumb am I, after trailing that sweetie of yours a thousand miles out of Center City. I suppose you deny shooting a telegram to Blondie before he croaked Chief Murdock back there. Just to remind you, it said, 'Pierce stuff the nuts answers are still soft be seeing you.'"

She shrank back at that, teeth sinking in her underlip. Her eyes went wild, furtive. I laughed through my teeth.

"Sort of hits home, eh? Well, get this, Blondie sapped a friend of mine, see? The croaking of Pierce here in K. C. is Flannery's worry. I want Blondie for the Center City job. The rest's by the way, as far as I'm concerned. If you're dirtied up with Pierce's death, well, tell it to Flannery. Stick a finger on Blondie and I'll be on my way."

Her red lips were a hard slashing line in the white face. The dark eyes were dull as glass. "No," she gritted.

I reached over, tapping the bare skin at the V of her gown. "Okay, then how will the rest of my yarn sound to the local bulls here? Blondie Spade climbed over an extension ladder from the roof of the Organ Building to Pierce's window. He knifed the lawyer and 'souped' the old iron can Pierce called a safe. He was after the Torquin rocks. Pierce was fencin' for him. What'd he sap Pierce for? Ask me another one. He was waitin' out on the Organ roof for the blow-off when I came into the room. The explosion knocked me out. Blondie came back into the room, got his rocks and lammed. And get this, made me out for the count on the floor."

Her dull eyes flicked with fascinated interest and I bored on.

"You phoned Pierce ten minutes later, checkin' up on the job. I answered that call. My voice worried you some. You and Kerrigan pulled a boner, framing me tonight. There was only one guy knew I was in town and that was Blondie Spade. He tipped you and Kerrigan who I was and you planned to iron me. Well, get this, sister, I'm hard to kill. The plant went haywire. Maybe you think I can't stick the squeeze on Kerrigan. I bought three decks of snow from his lousy joint tonight. Thanks to your tip off over the phone on the 'Cyprus' high sign. Maybe this all don't paint a picture for you—Blondie's headed for the hot squat right now. Make that. You'd better squawk fast if you want it to help any. I'm givin' you one more chance to talk. You spill now where I can find him or I'll take you to the bulls!"

She glowered sullenly into her lap. I waited a minute, then said, "Last call, Connie, what's the word?"

She didn't say anything.

I nodded, pivoted, went to the phone.

I said, "Police headquarters."

"My God!" she choked.

I covered the mouthpiece. "Want to talk yet, kid?"

Her smeary red lips drew into a straight line.

I barked, "Hello, Flannery there? Thanks. Put him on . . . Chief, Brandt Lennox speaking. Listen, I just broke free of a bad mix down at Kerrigan's Boat Club. Nosed in down there hoping to get word of Blondie Spade from the frail, Connie Lusk. It's a long yarn and I'll spill it in person. Right now, take a tip from me and sic a riot squad on that boat. It's a goofy joint and they're shoving dope there among other things . . .

"I got the dame with me at the hotel. I'll bring her along over. By the way, you might fan her apartment just in case it might build up the 'know' some. No. 349 Stockwell Avenue—got it from a letter here in her bag."

I hung up and slung down in a chair, building a pill. We waited half an hour. Connie didn't open her trap and I didn't say anything. I wanted to give Flannery time for the boat club pinch. Then I got up.

"Come on, kid," I says, "you've reneged. Now we're going places."

FLANNERY offered me a cigar. I shook my head and fished out a pill. We sat facing each other across his desk at headquarters. We were alone in the smoke-filled room. A fan rattled noisily on the window sill. It helped the stuffiness some.

"Not a thing on Blondie yet, I suppose?" I asked.

Flannery shook his head glumly. I'd just brought the facts up to date. They didn't look so promising, for me at least, sticking steel on Murdock's killer. We had the girl, sure, but was she a mum member? It looked like Blondie had hooked his loot and left. So far as we could tell, there wasn't a reason for sticking him in the K. C. If we could make Connie talk—but was that a crossword?

I scowled out into the hot night. Was her silence a stall for time to give the hop-head a clean pair of heels?

Flannery rose, creaking, from his chair, and took a turn round the room. I said, "Boys ought to be here soon on that Kerrigan pinch, Chief."

He nodded, parking again.

The door opened and the desk sergeant poked in a head.

"Logan's back from the jane's. Wanta see him, Chief?"

"Yes. Send him in."

The long lank detective I'd met that afternoon, stalked in carrying an alligator handbag. He nodded.

"It's Connie Lusk's," he explained. "She sure was all set to flit, from the looks of her apartment." He opened the bag and tossed two railroad tickets to the desk top. "She and the boy friend, I'm guessin'," he continued.

Flannery picked up the tickets. He grunted. " 'Frisco, eh?"

There came the pound of feet in the outer room. The sergeant appeared at the door again.

"Squad with Kerrigan, Chief."

"Wait!" barked Flannery, rising. "Have in Miss Lusk, Dan."

A few moments later Connie came through a side door, fathered by two coppers. She was still sullen and defiant. She slumped into a chair, sat biting her nails, staring at the floor. She had straightened herself up some, but the sleek beauty was gone. She looked hard, worn and tired.

Flannery crossed to the door. "Okay, Dan," he said, and came back round his desk.

Three blue boys pushed the disheveled form of Hooly Kerrigan into the room. His fat face was a flabby white. Tiny drops of moisture rode the corners of his lax mouth. His clothes were torn. His toupee had disappeared and an ugly welt glowed on his perfectly bald head. The officers slammed him into the chair across from the Chief.

"He was lammin' in a motor boat

when we blew up to the *Queen,*" said the man in a sergeant's uniform. "We tried grabbin' 'im and he pulled a gat on us. McCabe got it in the arm." He tossed a small black grip to the desk top, flipping back the lid. "Snow," he added. "Enough for a coupla states."

Flannery took one look. His face went grim as granite. "I'm not surprised," he remarked.

Kerrigan wet his lips and glared across at me, the Chief, the officers, and finally caught sight of Connie Lusk in the far corner.

He started. His face flushed a sullen red, then drained of color. His thick lips drew into a snarl.

"You!" he gritted. So—"

"So what?" she flared defiantly.

He made noises in his throat, swabbing at his thick lips. His darting eyes flicked about, returning to her white strained face.

"You—you—" he stuttered. "I wondered how the bulls tumbled. You lousy little 'crosser—"

"No," she choked, starting forward. "No—"

"Yeah? Well, why the hell should they pinch my joint then?"

"I— I—" she began.

"Kerrigan," I broke in softly, "don't be too hard on the dame. She was in a tough spot. If you hadn't pulled that K. O. game on me down at the Club tonight and given me a chance at her, she might never have cracked. Why, she even had two tickets bought for 'Frisco—her and the boy friend, I guess—" I let it go at that.

Kerrigan cursed, leaping forward. The coppers jerked him back. "I thought so," he growled. He raised cuffed hands, pointing an accusing finger at the cringing form of the girl. Words rose in his throat, spewed from his thick working lips. "Yellow," he sputtered. "I told Pierce so, warned him you'd tail on us the minute Spade hit town—"

"Shut up, you fool!" she screamed. "Can't you see—"

"Yeah, I can see!" he yelled. "You squawked when you got in a pinch. Thought you'd soften the spot for that damn' sweetie of yours—" He jerked round to Flannery. "Now maybe I can help some—" he panted. "Blondie Spade's been hiding out in the hold of my boat. When he blew in off that Torquin job I pulled a daddy to him, like a damn fool. This dame here insisted she'd get rid of him *pronto.*. Pierce was with her on it."

He ran a shaking hand across his mouth. "Blondie slipped Pierce the rocks to fence for 'em. That was three days ago when he blew in on Western Air. Pierce started stallin' Spade from the first. Claimed he had a soft spot in the Orient for the stuff. But that took time and Blondie wanted a quick turnover. I told Pierce it was dynamite—that hophead was restless. He'd sapped that copper in the east and might fly the coop any minute, spill his guts. To hell with profits and my piece of the take. I says to shuck the stuff, even give it back to Spade, but he soft pedalled that. That was yesterday, and now see what he got."

He paused, spread helpless hands and swabbed sweat from his face.

The men stood like statues in blue at his back. Connie was sitting very still, white as death, hard eyes searching Kerrigan's face. Flannery was hunched forward, hovering over his desk, keen eyes on the prisoner.

"I guess that'll hold her," Kerrigan blurted. "I may march through Georgia but I've fixed that double-crossin' dame fer good and I hope to God you spike that snow sniffer."

"You rat!" Connie leaped from her chair. "Well, get this. I didn't spill one damn word. Not even when Lennox here thirded me at the Mulbach. But now I'm talkin." She whirled on Flannery.

"Backed by Grant Pierce, this palooka's been shoving dope at his boat for over a year! Gets the stuff from the Chink, Wong Gee, head of the dope ring up in Saint Jo. His supply comes down river from there at midnight, Thursdays. He keeps tabs on the Federals and meets the Chink's launch off Midway Island. They transfer there. Lennox, here, can check the 'know' on that even if your men hadn't hooked Kerrigan's black suitcase. He bought three decks across the table at the *Cypress Queen* tonight before the dumb waiter tumbled to who he was."

She whirled on Kerrigan, white-faced, and sunken low in his chair. "You poor fool," she sobbed. "I didn't double-cross you. You—you sap, you spilled a mouthful—" She turned, sobbing, toward her chair.

I said, "Wipe your nose clean, kid. We won't forget it. Where's Blondie Spade?"

Triumph gleamed in her eyes as she whirled on me. "Try and find him," she clipped, closing her lips like a trap.

I shrugged.

"Take 'em away, boys," Flannery jerked a grizzled head toward his men. They trooped out with their prisoners.

"Whew!" I grinned. "That *was* a hunch, bringin' 'em together, eh, Chief?"

He nodded. "What price Blondie Spade now?" I asked.

He shook his head. "God knows. She might break under more pressure but my guess is not."

CHAPTER VI

Lost Loot

TEN minutes later, I stood in the middle of Pierce's office where the tragedy had occurred. The feet of the janitor sounded off down the hall. The windows were closed. The place was stuffy. I crossed over, raised the curtain to the court window and ran up the sash. Night air rushed in. It felt good. Across the steel landing of the fire escape the black roof of the Organ Building loomed.

I turned, staring at the plant stand. It had been sudden memory of a written address on the small table there that suggested the visit, while I was tromping up Fourteenth street toward my hotel. The billing tag lay exposed to view beside the shoe box packed with cactus. It read:

Wong Gee Tea House, Inc.

Saint Joseph, Mo.

I got to wondering what the hell Pierce would be shipping cactus up there for. Maybe the Chink dope shover, masking under the reputable business of wholesaling tea, was also a plant connoisseur. Maybe not. Pierce had been busy wrapping up the shipment when he was killed, just before I blew in.

That, and dictating. My puzzled frown rose from contemplation of the innocent looking box and shifted to the dictaphone. I recalled now shutting it off. Dust had settled on the black disc record. I reached down and turned the lever on to "play." There came the customary scratching, then a voice broke the stillness:

Mr. Wong Gee, President,
Wong Gee Tea House, Inc.,
St. Joseph, Mo.

Dear Greer:
Am shipping under separate cover two dozen mushroom cactus plants as per our conversation over long distance last night.
Am not forgetting your kindness in this affair and needless to say it was a relief to me to know that you could handle it.
As usual, deposit credit for same in First National there. We can work out details after consignment has been placed with people in Yokohama.
Relative to the—

The calm voice broke off. There came blurred sounds, then a sudden gasp, muttering faintly, "Blondie—what the hell—don't. Put up that knife—" a sputtering, a deep groan, grinding silence.

I snapped the lever grimly. If I'd wanted final evidence that Blondie Spade was Pierce's killer, here it was in a nut shell. But why all the hokus pokus about the cactus plants, a consignment to far off Yokohama through Wong Gee, deposit of credit in the St. Jo bank?

I crossed to the table, stared curiously down at the neatly rowed plants wedged side by side in their pasteboard container. Common variety enough, certainly. Not over two bits a dozen for such stuff in the southwest.

Taking the pen, I snaked out one of the squat, prickly bulbs. It rolled on its side. I stared at the stem spot. The next instant I'd whipped out a pen knife and was digging at the thing. It lifted free like a cork in a bottle.

I up-ended the plant. Light flashed in my eyes. There was something bright inside.

I hacked at the thing, sharp spines gouging my fingers. A diamond rolled out, the size of a finger nail!

I'd found the secret of the Torquin loot! There were two more gems wedged in the green bedding. A second and third plant disclosed several more. I guessed the remainder of that hundred grand in loot was under my hand.

Contrary to my belief, Blondie had been too late blowing the safe. Pierce himself must have taken the gems that had rested there and transferred them to his plants. That changed the picture. If Blondie had scrammed K. C. he'd done so without the Torquin haul.

There was a faint noise at the open window. I whirled, a cactus bulb still clutched in my hand. I was staring into the black nose of an automatic!

There on the sill, a twisted snarl on his over-white face, crouched Blondie Spade. He wore dirty unionalls, a ragged felt rode his narrow, glittering eyes. The left one jerked spasmodically. Sweat gleamed on his upper lip, free of its mustache now. The hop had a yen clawing his vitals. The gat wobbled in his nervous fingers.

He spoke low, gratingly. "Thanks for finding the junk, louse. Now take something to remember me by."

I sensed his tugging trigger finger and dropped to my knees, hurling the prickly plant straight at his eyes. His gat bellowed and his choked yell rode the echo as the spines sank in the flesh of his cheek.

He fired again, wildly, clawing at his face. Lead smacked the wall, the glass door. Then my own palmed rod spoke twice in thundering succession, and he toppled backward, cursing. I lunged forward, watching, catlike, while he thrashed around on the escape landing.

Suddenly he clawed upright. Teeth bared in a snarl, white face working with hate, he loosed more lead. My hat jerked free of my head. I reeled back, shooting from the hip.

Blondie screamed curses, tossing his arms above his head. He whirled part way round, teetered an instant over the railing, then plunged over, hurtling from sight. His long agonized yell echoed hollowly in the court well.

A GIRL'S sleepy voice said, "Yes?" She was on the Western Union end of the Chief's wire at H. Q. I stuck lips close to the receiver and said:

"Straight message for Acting Chief Gorky, Police Headquarters, Center City, Pa. Get that? . . . Okay. 'BLONDIE SPADE IN THE SOCK STOP KILLED SCRAMMING MY LEAD IN PIERCE'S OFFICE STOP TORQUIN LOOT RECOVERED INTACT LETTER FOLLOWS.' Signed Brandt Lennox."

I hung up. Flannery grinned back at me over his desk through fuming stogie smoke. Dawn fingered at the windows. I'd dug him out of bed for the story. The box of cactus lay between us under the desk lamp.

Beyond a closed door and down a corridor, Blondie Spade lay very quiet on a slab, staring at the ceiling.

Flannery said, "Right under our noses, eh?" He was looking at the shoe box.

I grunted, pawing for a smoke. "You a movie fan, Chief?"

"Movie?" he asked. "What in blazes—?"

I grinned. "There's a little one-reeler at the Regent called 'Easy Pickens.' I'll stake you to the show tomorrow if you'll come along."

He stared quizzically. "Sure," he said. "Not that I get the connection but if you say it's good—" he waved a hand. "A cop needs relaxation once in a while."

"Relaxation?" I laughed, rising. "That film'll give you the headache and I'll buy the aspirin. We'll hit the first matinée."

I made for the door.

"What's it about?" he yelled as I swung out.

"A fanned poke, some hot ice and a cop with a dirty nose," I answered.

I left on his "What the bloody hell!"

LUGER LAW

By RICHARD E. CONAN

CHAPTER I

The Pedretti Plates

MY voice was slow and even. I said:

"This is a stick-up, gents!"

The sound of the press died with a whir. The heads of the three shirt-sleeved gents behind it snapped erect. They stared down the long barrel of my Luger.

I straddled my legs, balanced myself on the balls of my feet, reached behind me and closed the door as silently as I had opened it. From behind the slits of the domino that covered the upper half of my face, I watched them narrowly.

Lazarus stood in the middle, heavy-set, swarthy, his head as nude as a billiard ball. Marling stood on his right; Kinsetta on his left. Just three of the boys—three of the big boys. I knew them well and that's where the breaks were all mine. They would have given a small fortune to have seen the face behind the mask; to have known the name of the lad who held the gun.

As a matter of fact, it happens to be Kilday.

I said sharply: "Put 'em up and behind your heads!"

Slowly, mechanically, they obeyed, warily eyeing the Luger. But I had seen too many rods—both from behind and from in front—to make any mistakes. You make mistakes like that only once, and I had survived in the racket for a long time.

I gave the place a swift once-over. It could have been the living room of any one of a thousand Philadelphia homes—save for one difference. And it was that difference that interested me—the long, zinc-covered table that stood between me and Lazarus, Kinsetta and Marling.

Mounted on one end of it was a small hand-press of the latest model and design. Ranged down one side were bottles of special inks—red, blue and black; and opposite these were stacks of special bonded horsehair paper—paper of the kind and quality that is used for making bank notes.

I had cased the set-up from every angle. I knew all about it.

My eyes were narrowed, my hand steady on the gun as I rummaged in a pocket for a package of cigarettes. I shook a butt half out of the packet, flipped it to the corner of my mouth and thumbed a match to flame. I lit up carefully, then with two streams of smoke curling down beneath the domino, I said:

"Yes, gents. This is one of the things you read about in the tab sheets."

Two patches of sweat made irregular circles in the arm-pits of Lazarus' shirt. I saw the heavy muscles bulge beneath his sleeve bands, saw the muscles of his stomach tense and flex beneath their rolls of fat.

He said nastily: "Sure. Just like they do in the movies. What are you waiting for, bright boy?"

I grinned. "Assistance, sweetheart," I said sweetly. "Assistance."

Lazarus' eyes narrowed. Beads of sweat made a halo around the rim of his bald head. He fought to control the anger in his voice when he spoke again.

"Christ, fella, you can't get away with this!"

I tapped the ashes off the butt with my left forefinger, hefted the Luger comfortably in my right fist. I said politely: "No? Why not?"

Lazarus' right hand was edging down to the gun strapped under his armpit. The Luger jerked steady in my fist and my voice was sharp and acid. "I wouldn't try it, sweetheart," I advised. "This is a gun—it goes boom-boom—and it hurts like hell. Keep 'em up!"

The three pairs of hands slowly reached for the ceiling again. A moment later they froze there. Strained, rapt expressions came over the faces of the three. The bristles at the base of Lazarus' skull were moist and clammy; Marling and Kinsetta were breathing slow and deep. Their eyes fixed on the door behind my back with a concentrated stare. For a footstep had sounded down the corridor beyond.

I grinned crookedly and shook my head.

"At ease, boys," I said. "Don't excite yourselves. That's only my assistance. After we put your loogan away he prowled the joint while I entertained you three."

The door opened and a second masked figure entered the room—Joe Bassett. The gun in his hand matched the one in mine.

Joe said laconically: "Bag!"

I echoed him: "Bag here!"

Lazarus smiled crookedly. "It's a nice routine, boys," he said patiently. "We like it fine. But you're crazy as hell if you think you can get away with it." His voice took on a conversational, patronizing tone and as he spoke he began to slowly edge down his hands. "You boys have spent a lot of time rehearsing the act. It's swell. But if you're wise, you'll take fifty grand and forget all about it."

I laughed shortly, said: "Fifty grand from those plates?"

Lazarus nodded slowly. "You never saw better green goods."

I scratched my left ear, said with an abstracted air: "That's what they tell me. That's why we rehearsed the act. That's why the stick up. If you can make twenty dollar bills from the Pedretti plates and pass 'em at par, we'd be suckers to pass 'em up for a chiselling fifty grand. The answer is no, sweetheart! It's no deal." I nodded to Bassett, spoke from the corner of my mouth. "Take 'em away!"

Bassett dropped his Luger into the pocket of his coat, brought out instead a heavy roll of adhesive tape. Lazarus and the other two watched him from hot eyes; I watched Lazarus, Marling and Kinsetta.

Bassett moved forward pulling a strip from the roll of tape. Then he made a sap play! My shout of warning was a fraction of a second too late! Bassett walked between me and the three shirt-sleeved gents!

I FLUNG myself sideways and squeezed the trigger of the Luger as Lazarus threw himself backward and down behind the table.

Lead criss-crossed the room. I felt something hot and acid sting me in the left shoulder; felt something warm that ran crazily down my bare arm.

Bassett cursed savagely as fire belched from behind the zinc-lined table. Marling and Kinsetta stood frozen for a split second. I jumped fast along the wall. Behind the table, Lazarus' heavy face tensed, his gun crashed again. Then my Luger smashed out and a slug grooved Lazarus' bald dome.

Lazarus lurched forward onto his knees, went down slow, squeezed lead again. The impact of the shot spun me back against the wall. More blood ran crazily down my dead left arm.

The smile was off my lips. I mouthed a short, bitter curse, steadied myself. The Luger jerked to avid life—spoke twice—very rapidly.

Lazarus' gun arm came up. His automatic sailed in a wide arc towards the ceiling, crashed with a metallic clatter in the far corner of the room. Then he collapsed forward on his face, buckled up his knees, straightened them out again and lay very still. Marling and Kinsetta turned white.

I said evenly to Bassett: "Tape up those mugs, and fast. We got two minutes to get away from here."

Joe grunted bitterly: "I'll do better than that!"

He stepped over to Marling. The barrel of his Luger rose and fell. Marling took it without batting an eye. His knees buckled and he kissed the floor.

Kinsetta said: "You rats! You'll never . . ."

Joe's Luger choked the words in his throat as it creased his skull. Kinsetta went down to join Marling and Lazarus on the floor.

We got away from there well within two minutes. And with us went the Pedretti plates.

CHAPTER II

Under Cover

WITH my elbow crooked casually out of the open window on my left, I drove the black Chrysler sedan at an even twenty-five miles per hour down Broad Street. I handled the bus carefully, driving neither too fast nor too slow. At my side sat Bassett, nursing a gun on his knees.

At the corner of Market the light went red against us. I pulled up at the intersection alongside a traffic cop. I lit a cigarette with steady fingers, extinguished the match with a flick of my wrist and dropped it over the side of the car.

The light flashed green and I got away from there. At Chestnut I turned left and a minute later pulled up at the curb at the corner of Fourteenth.

I said to Bassett: "There'll be a stink, Joe. We better keep under cover for a while."

Bassett growled sourly, said: "*They* can't make a stink."

I shook my head back and forth, pursed my lips in a soundless whistle. "No," I admitted. "Not much of a one. But that gun play is going to bring not only the dicks but the Federal Cops into the picture. Not so hot!"

Bassett said: "What's the lay?"

I answered: "I figure we're in the clear but there's no use taking any chances. We'll lay low at Morehouse's for a while till the fuss blows over. Then we'll know what to do."

Bassett agreed. We each took one of the Pedretti plates. Sure, we were pals—sure, we had pulled the job together! But those plates together spelled a fortune. What the hell—you know how it is. Joe was a nice lad and all that but both of us felt better, each one of us hanging on to one of the plates.

He got out of the car and faded. I shifted into gear again, bucked traffic once more and a few minutes later pulled up at the Pennsy Station.

At the check room I bummed a sheet of wrapping paper and some heavy cord, wrapped up my plate and checked it. Then, as an added precaution I mailed the check to myself, care of General Delivery.

My left arm was beginning to give me hell. I went out to the car again.

A half hour later I pulled up before a modern, tapestry-brick apartment on Kenwood Avenue. I parked the car, got out and walked into the building. The lobby was empty. All to the good. I got into the automatic elevator, rode to the fourth floor, got out and walked down a thick-piled carpet to the south wing of the building.

I stopped before apartment 4D, fitted a key into the lock and went on inside.

Mona was waiting for me—as she always did. Mona was the goods. Class! A man never had a gamer, squarer dame. I thought a hell of a lot about Mona—more than she ever suspected; more than I ever told her, I guess.

She studied my face closely as I ripped off my coat. Her eyes went wide when she saw the blood-stained shirt beneath.

"What happened?" she said.

"Get to work on this," I answered.

The kid was 'way ahead of me. When she came out of the bathroom a minute later with a basin of water, iodine and bandages, she said again: "What happened?"

"Lazarus stopped lead," I answered.

"So what?"

"He's dead."

"What happened?"

I shrugged. "Get a knife and dig out that lead. There're two slugs." I lit a cigarette as she worked on my arm. "Joe pulled a dumb play. Walked between my gun and Lazarus'. There were fireworks. Nice routine while it lasted. Lazarus looked funny as hell as he kissed the floor."

Mona worked out the two slugs with a penknife, swabbed the holes with iodine and made a good job of a bandage. While she patted it into place, she asked another question.

"Did you get what you went after?"

I nodded. "Joe's got one and I've got the other."

While the kid cleaned up the mess I went into the bedroom and changed clothes. I came out a few minutes later with my undershirt, shirt, and suit rolled up in a ball. I said: "Get rid of these, babe," and reached for my hat.

Mona looked at me with surprised eyes. "Where are you going?" she asked.

"Joe and I are going to lay low for a while," I told her. "At Eddie Morehouse's. I'm pretty sure we're in the clear but there's no use taking chances. If anybody *should* come around, you don't know anything, see? I'm in Chi on business. Been away a week. And if you want to reach me in a hurry—call Eddie. Got it?"

Mona nodded. A little frown of worry puckered her brows. She started to ask another question, then changed her mind. Good kid, Mona. I smiled, walked over to her and placed my two hands on her bare shoulders.

"Take it easy, babe," I said. "The stink will blow over. Nothing to worry about."

She smiled up at me and said: "Sure."

She pressed her body close to mine, kissed me hard on the lips, broke away and said: "Don't make it too long."

THERE was a stink, all right. A big stink. Worse than we had expected. The Federal cops must have had their finger on Lazarus for a long time. With an eye to re-election, the D. A. took a personal interest in his passing. The Police Commissioner wanted the glory for himself. And as a result, they all tangled. Federals, Squad men and the D. A.'s special agents got in each other's hair, tripped over each other's feet and called each other a lot of nasty names.

But more important, the finger was never pointed at us.

In our room on the third floor back of Morehouse's joint Basset and I read the papers and laughed like hell. The front pages of the tab sheets were plastered with a mournful looking photograph of Lazarus. Funny as hell. The photo had been carefully retouched and the result was a riot. His fat face leered up from the limp page like some bloated, unbelievable cherub.

The captions were even more maudlin. But they left me cold. No one really cried his heart out over the passing of fat-bellied Lazarus and I wasn't shedding any tears myself.

Five days went by. A love nest murder crowded Lazarus off the front page. A platinum blonde, her hard features beautified by the same artistic photographer, stole his place of honor. The press had something new to squawk about and the cops, with plenty of noise and gusto, promptly tackled this more promising case.

All to the good.

Another day went by and I gave the nod to Bassett. We were getting sick of Morehouse's lousy whiskey, getting sick of each other and of ourselves. It was good to get out again.

CHAPTER III

The Heat

ONCE more I parked the car before the apartment house on Kenwood Avenue. I crawled from behind the wheel and Joe followed me across the sidewalk to the door. I felt the nuts; felt like a groom on his wedding night. It would be good to see the kid again. Funny how that girl had gotten under my skin! I had missed her a lot.

I fitted the key into the door of 4D and swung the door open. Joe followed me across the threshold. A stale, musty air crinkled in my nostrils. I frowned, looked puzzled—felt a funny, tightening feeling around my heart.

I called out: "Mona!"

No answer.

I looked at Joe. "I guess she's not here," I said dumbly.

Joe shrugged, grinned, said: "A wise guy let's 'em know when he's going to call."

I growled him down. Of one thing I was sure—and that was that the kid wouldn't two-time me. I started down the hall with a long stride and the further I got the more leery I became. Not leery, exactly—not leery of danger or gun-play. It was something else. Something that kept beating in my heart and brain! Something that told me that things were screwy as hell.

The apartment was quiet as a tomb. I had never heard it so quiet. Joe's feet and mine echoed hollowly against the walls.

I called, "Mona!" again.

No answer.

Joe laughed, a short, uneasy laugh. He said: "Christ, that's funny!"

I whirled on him. "What's funny?"

He swung his head from side to side, looked over his shoulder. He said slowly: "This dump reminds me of the morgue."

I snarled at him. "For Christ sake, shut up."

But all the time I knew that Joe had expressed the feeling that had been eating at my heart. The living room was empty and in order. I tried the bathroom next—the kitchenette—and all the time I was asking myself why I was fighting shy of the bedroom.

I crossed to the door slowly, slowly swung it open. Joe crowded behind me as I felt for the light switch. The lights exploded in the room like a bomb.

Behind me Joe whispered hoarsely: "Christ!"

I couldn't say anything, do anything, move. My guts tangled into a hard knot. My mouth was hot; my eyes hot. My heart pounded once against my ribs like a hammer, then stopped still. For there on the bed lay Mona—and I knew that she was dead!

More—I knew that she had been murdered!

Behind me Joe said "Christ!" again.

Something clicked in my mind—my heart started pumping again. I moved forward automatically.

She lay on her back wrapped in a flimsy negligee. One knee was buckled up under her; the other bare leg dangled grotesquely over the edge of the unmade bed. Her blue eyes were wide and staring, the irises distended. A gag, made from one of her silk stockings, was still stuffed in her mouth. One end of it slopped down over her chin. Her skin was puffy and purple.

For a long minute I stared at that face—the face that was Mona's and yet somehow, wasn't. I was dumb. The iron fist round my guts began to twist. I felt suddenly sick. Sweat popped out on my forehead; my hands trembled.

I wanted to bellow with rage; I wanted to do something violent. I locked my teeth together, dug my nails deep into the palms of my clenched fists.

And then the frenzy was gone. Ice water flowed in my veins. My brain was hot but clear.

Joe said in a whisper: "Who in the hell could have done that?"

I shook my head. When I spoke, the calmness of my voice surprised me. I said: "I don't know, Joe—yet. But when I do . . ."

My voice trailed off. With an effort I moved my staring eyes from Mona's. Slowly they travelled down her face, stopped at her throat. The flesh was bruised and swollen and the finger-prints of the man who had strangled her stood out brutally against the creamy satin of her negligee.

Her arms and legs were a welter of livid scars. Glowing cigarette butts, smouldering cigar stubs had made those marks. Mona's flesh! The stench of the burning was strong in my nostrils.

Gently I took the gag from her mouth, straightened her out on the bed. Gently I closed her eyes.

Suddenly I stooped down, picked up a paper packet of matches from the floor. On the back was an ad for Eddie Frandzen's *Parfait Club* in New York.

I turned to Joe.

I said: "Let's scram!"

"Christ!" said Joe. "I need a drink."

WE talked it over at the nearest bar. It was a cinch to figure out. I could see it all as if I had been there. Mona had been in bed—the bell had rung. Figuring it was me she had gone to the door. Someone had forced his way in at the point of a gun. Two—three, maybe.

And there was only one question

they could have asked her; only one question that could have accounted for the torture act. And that was: *Where had I hid the Pedretti plates!* Poor kid! She didn't know—she couldn't tell 'em.

And so they had killed her!

That packet of matches from the *Parfait Club!* I did a hell of a lot of thinking about that—from more than one angle.

When the dicks got through with me I buried Mona.

After the funeral Joe and I spent an hour in silence over a bottle of Scotch. When the bottle was empty I said: "I'm going to New York, Joe."

He ground his butt out beneath his heel before answering. Then: *"Parfait Club?"*

I nodded.

Joe grunted. "I've a friend there — Salvy Benetti — Frandzen's manager. You know—one of those things. I did him a favor once. Play it for what it's worth."

I got up, shrugged myself into my coat, said: "Thanks, Joe. Maybe I will. You stick here in Philly. Keep your eye on things. If anything breaks that you think I ought to know, write me—or get in touch with me through Benetti. I got a hunch I'll be around the *Parfait Club* a lot."

Joe ordered a small beer, then said to me: "What about the—"

I cut him short. "You got yours and I got mine. That can wait. I got a job to do first."

CHAPTER IV

The Parfait Club

I WAS always pretty hard; I always knew how to take care of myself. But unlike lots of mugs in the racket I had never gotten gun-drunk. True, I had plugged a man on more than one occasion. But I had never gotten a hell of a kick out of it. It was a case of take it—or give it. And I had usually managed to give it.

Now, I was all washed up with that. When I stepped off the train at New

York I was a hair trigger killer. I was out to get the rats that had given Mona the business—and the sooner and bloodier, the better.

I checked in at the Bellmore at ten. At eleven I checked my hat with the girl at the *Parfait Club.* I went on in through the heavy draped archway that led to the main floor of the club.

For a moment I stood in the doorway and surveyed the joint. Business was good. The tables were crowded beneath subdued rose shaded lamps, the oval shaped dance floor was packed. The jazz band was banging out a syncopated version of *Bolero.*

A week ago I would have gotten a kick out of taking a twirl at the bright lights. Now, it was so much horse-feathers to me.

A perspiring head waiter bustled up to me.

"Table for one, sir. There's a—"

I cut him short with: "Later, John. First, I want to see Benetti. Tell him a gent from Philly."

He gave me a shrewd look, hesitated.

I said: "On your way, bright-boy.

Benetti—I want to see him—a gent from Philly."

He swallowed at his Adam's apple, mumbled a thick, "Yes, sir," and headed for a door on my left which was decorated with a sign marked PRIVATE.

I watched him go in without knocking. By the time I had lit up a cigarette he was out again. He motioned to me with his head. I walked over to the door.

He said: "Mr. Benetti's inside. You're to go in."

Salvy Benetti, the manager of Frandzen's *Parfait Club,* looked up as I entered. He had small blue eyes, thin, washed-out straw-colored hair. He had fat jowls, packed too much fat around his waist and too many diamonds on his hands.

We sized each other up for an instant. He didn't look any too healthy to me and I guess he felt the same way about yours truly. But that was no skin off my rear end. Bassett had put the okay on him and that was enough.

I said: "The name's Kilday."

Benetti smiled thinly, wrapped his pudgy hands around his middle and tilted back in his chair. He shook his head, said: "I don't make the name."

I shrugged. "I don't go in for front page publicity," I said. "Unless there's an accident."

Benetti pursed his lips and said: "Ah!" Then conversationally: "Philly's a nice town."

I said: "Yes." This guy Benetti wasn't as dumb as he looked. Then I went on. "Joe Bassett told me to look you up."

That registered. Benetti showed a spark of interest. "Joe's a nice fella," he said. "What can I do for you?"

"I might be getting a letter from Joe," I answered. "It'll come to me through you. I'd appreciate—"

Benetti waved the words aside with a diamond studded hand. "Sure, why not?" he said. He pulled open the top drawer of his desk, extracted a bottle of Bourbon and two glasses. He poured the drinks carefully, shoved one across to me.

I picked up my glass, said: "That's not all."

Benetti paused with his glass half way to his lips.

"No? What else?" he asked, arching his brows.

"I want a knock-down to Vee Gorman," I told him.

Benetti frowned. "Can do; but that's not so hot."

"No?" I asked politely. "Why?"

Benetti ran a pudgy hand down one side of his face. "The Gorman frail is Frandzen's red-hot. You know how it is. Eddie hangs out the 'Hands-off' sign. He's touchy as hell about her."

I THOUGHT of Mona. My eyes got hard and my jaw set. "I don't blame him," I said. "But I'll risk it. I'll have a table in a corner. Have your pusher send the girl over."

Benetti said: "Okay."

I downed my drink, said, "Thanks," and started for the door.

I spotted Vee Gorman as she threaded her way through the maze of tables, headed in my direction. I saw her wide blue eyes as she looked about her—eyes that were hauntingly like Mona's. I felt lousy as hell. I swallowed a funny lump in my throat and tried to shut out the memory.

She pulled up at my table, looked down at me with questioning eyes. She said: "You wanted to see me?"

I nodded, stood up and kicked out a chair for her. "Yes," I said slowly. "Better sit down."

Her brows went up, she shrugged, then slipped into the chair.

"So what?" she asked.

"I'm Kilday," I told her. I looked at her briefly, then out at the crowded dance floor. It was going to be harder than I had thought. I had a neat little speech all framed for the occasion but at the show-down my brain was reduced to a dull aching void.

I turned back to her. I gave it to her straight.

"Mona's dead," I said in a hard voice.

She stiffened as if some one had slugged her. The color drained from her face. For a moment I thought she was going to pass out. But she was game. She could take it. Her knuckles showed white on clenched fists and her eyes closed for a moment. Then slowly they opened. She drew a deep breath, asked hoarsely:

"When—how?"

"Two-three days ago," I said. "Bumped!"

My words must have stunned her. She looked at me, dumb-like, as if she couldn't believe it. She shook her head a little as if she were trying to shake off the effects of a blow. Then slowly hot color flamed to her cheeks. She leaned far across the table. Her voice trembled.

"For God's sake, who—and why?"

My brain was crystal clear again. Once more the cold, ruthless instinct of the killer possessed me. I looked around the crowded club.

I said bitterly: "The answer's here. I'll find the rat—and when I do—"

She knew all the answers. The kid had guts. Her hand closed over my own. Her fingers were like cold steel.

She said in a hard voice: "This is my party, too, Kilday! What do I do?"

I lit a butt slowly, studied her face. It wasn't so lovely now. The eyes were hard, her mouth tight, and twin pulses beat violently in her creamy throat.

I said: "Sit tight. Keep your eyes and ears open and your mouth shut!"

She nodded, looked through me and beyond me. Then I saw her stiffen. I followed her gaze, saw a tall man whose wide shoulders bulged the jacket of his tuxedo, whose wavy blond hair topped a face that might have been carved from granite.

He made straight for our table, glanced briefly at the girl, then turned expressionless green eyes on me. I stared back, felt instinctively that the girl was suddenly nervous, ill at ease. For no definite reason I felt sore.

Vee Gorman spoke, a trifle hurriedly. "Eddie, this is a friend of mine. His name is—"

She hesitated a fraction of a second, looked at me. I filled in the void.

"Kilday," I said. Then slowly, as an afterthought: "Kilday from Philadelphia."

It didn't register with Frandzen. He nodded curtly. I drummed my fingers on the table top and held his eyes with my own. He turned away from me, stared down at the girl.

"The car's outside. As soon as you're through with Kilday—"

He strode off. It sounded more like an order than an invitation to me. Mentally I chalked up Eddie Frandzen as ice—ice and dynamite. I didn't think I was going to get along with Frandzen any too well. Not that it worried me any. I didn't care how big they came—how hard they were—what their connections were! If they had anything to do with—

Vee Gorman scraped back her chair. "I've got to be going." She stood up, took a step away from the table, then hesitated. "Don't mind Eddie," she explained. "That's his way. He's a swell guy when you know him."

I grunted noncommittally. "Maybe he is," I said slowly, "but what I said about keeping your mouth shut goes for *everybody.*"

She frowned slightly, then nodded. I saw her lips harden as she turned and made her way across the floor.

I hung around the *Parfait Club* for another half hour, had two Manhattans and did a lot of thinking. I figured the Gorman kid was on the up and up. But I couldn't say that I was crazy about the company she was keeping.

Benetti, the manager of the *Parfait,* was too slick for my straightforward disposition. Frandzen didn't look like he had a heart of gold.

But that was no skin off me.

I began to think about Mona. I felt lousy. I had a shot of Scotch straight, called for my check and got out.

Out on the street I hesitated a moment, lit a cigarette and debated whether I should walk back to the hotel or take a cab. And then I stopped worrying about such trifles.

A big black sedan was parked up the street about twenty feet away from me. Now, as I flipped my match into the gutter it got under way and began to move down on me. I gave it but a glance and didn't tumble. Must have been thinking about Mona.

Then a dame behind me screamed! My head snapped up just in time to see the ugly snout of a sub-machine gun jammed out the window of the car.

I dropped to one knee, rolled back towards the building and into the darkness of a narrow alley-way as the Tommy-gun went to work. It leaped to life with a brittle skeleton's rattle. Orange flame spewed from its nozzle.

Lead bounded off the pavement at my feet, ricocheted off the sandstone face of the club. Then the range was elevated. I rolled along some more. Stone splinters chewed into my face.

The push of night revellers that had been on the sidewalk a moment before faded.

My Luger glistened under the incandescents of the *Parfait Club.* I squeezed lead, grinned, squeezed lead again and heard the tinkle of breaking glass as the windshield of the car went out.

The traffic cop on the corner raised hell on his whistle. He came a-running, shooting—just shooting!

The sedan stopped. The Tommy-gun was roaring. I was flat on my belly, my nose in the dust. And believe it or not, I wasn't sore. In fact, I was tickled to death. This little shooting fray, now that it was practically over, meant a hell of a lot to me. It meant that if I was on the spot—I was on the right track!

Abruptly it seemed that all life on Broadway had died. Only the flickering lights of the electric signs overhead continued to beat down like a thousand spotlights. There was an unnatural hush of night noises broken only by the now slower rattle of the Tommy-gun and the growl of my answering Luger.

Lead whistled over my head, fanned my check. Close—too close! I cursed, kept on rolling and jammed a fresh clip into my gun.

The car was under way again.

Then suddenly the bated breath of Broadway came to life with a bang. Women screamed; broken glass tinkled, then crashed; taxis honked their horns furiously.

The sedan roared by me, sideswiped the cop who was charging down on the scene. That was my cue. I made the most of it. A Yellow cab came shooting by. I made the running board in one leap.

I poked my Luger under the driver's nose, said: "Keep rolling, buddy!"

He kept rolling.

At Sixth Avenue I flung him a bill, changed cabs, was jerked down to Penn Station. Here I grabbed a subway to Fourteenth Street, got out and then took a local uptown.

Everything was rosy at the hotel when I got there.

A week passed.

CHAPTER V

Frandzen Barges In

THERE was a knock on the door. I was expecting it. I put down my drink, got up, patted the butt of my Luger and crossed to the portal.

But I was only half expecting what I saw when I opened the door. I saw Frandzen on the threshold, backed by one of his wipers. I saw twin automatics glinting in their fists. My eyebrows went up. I grinned crookedly, said:

"Backed by that I can't do anything but invite you in."

Frandzen didn't crack a smile. His face was frozen ice. He said icily: "We're coming in without an invite."

I said: "Sure—why not," conversationally. Then straight in Frandzen's teeth: "You're not so tough, big boy."

Without giving him a chance for a come-back, I turned my back on him, crossed the room again and picked up my unfinished drink. Frandzen followed me in. His wiper closed the door, stood with his back to it.

I jerked my head in the general direction of the bottle. "Have a drink?" I said. "Pretty lousy stuff. But you ought to be used to it. It came out of the *Parfait Club.*"

Frandzen's expression never changed. He hefted the gat in his hand, looked around my hotel room.

"Lose something?" I asked politely.

Frandzen turned slowly to me. His eyes were green agates. His mouth was nasty. He said: "I don't lose women, Kilday."

I shrugged, poured myself another drink. "Just the answer to a virgin's prayer, eh? I'm not interested, Frandzen."

His eyebrows flicked rapidly, twice.

He jammed his gun forward, buried the point of it in my navel.

"I don't make you, Kilday," he said. "What's your racket?"

Our eyes met, held. I said evenly: "Death's my racket!"

The corner of Frandzen's hard mouth twitched in a smile, then was still. His gun sank another notch into my gut.

"Just how do you want me to take that?" he asked.

I never backed up, my eyes never left his. I said: "If you're the rat I'm looking for there's only one way to take it. If you're not—forget it.

If it means anything to you—shoot and shoot fast."

He stared at me for a long moment from unblinking eyes. Then he shook his head slowly.

"It doesn't mean a damn thing to me. The only way I can figure you is that you're nuts. But I don't like nuts running around with my women!"

I smiled with my lips, said: "So that's what's bothering you—the Gorman kid?" He didn't answer. I said impatiently: "Don't be a chump, Frandzen. Vee Gorman don't mean a damn thing to me—that way. She's a swell kid—she wouldn't look at another guy but you. She—"

Frandzen cut me short.

"Nuts! She's been doing plenty of looking at you the past week. You got two minutes, Kilday, to explain and explain right."

I said wearily: "Christ! This heavy lover stuff! You've been seeing too many movies, Frandzen. I tell you the kid is on the up and up. She wouldn't two-time you for John Gilbert."

"Make mine strawberry," said Frandzen in a bored voice. "That doesn't explain why she's so interested in you."

My eyes narrowed, my voice hardened. "She's not interested in me," I said. "She's interested in the thing I'm after!"

"And that is?"

"You've got all the answers right now," I said. "Take it or leave it!"

Frandzen's eyes never flickered, his frozen face never changed. His voice was emotionless when he said: "I'm leaving it! I don't like you, Kilday—I don't like anything about you." Then, over his shoulder to his loogan: "Take him, Al."

"Just like that, eh?" I said.

Then three things happened almost simultaneously. The wiper obediently headed in my direction. I got set for gun play and then the door to the can burst open. Vee Gorman stood in the opening. A .32 automatic glinted in her hand. She said: "Don't draw, Al!"

She came forward into the room slowly. The wiper looked at her, leered, then turned to Frandzen.

"Keerist, what a set-up!" he said.

The girl brushed him aside, went up to Frandzen, said: "Don't be a chump, Eddie!"

He looked down at her, his eyes a slaty gray, his face bleak. His lips were hard. "That settles it," he clipped out.

Vee Gorman laughed in his face. Then all of a sudden she changed tactics. She tossed her gat to the nearest chair, stepped back from Frandzen, put her hands on her hips and looked scornfully up at him.

"Okay by me, big boy. Go ahead—make a damn fool of yourself, if you want to."

It worked. A long breath whistled out of my lungs. A faint tinge of color crept into Frandzen's granite features.

"Maybe," he said, "but no dame's going to make one out of me."

The kid shook her head soberly. "Nobody's trying to," she said. "It's just like Kilday said. Everything's on the up and up as far as you're concerned. There's no use dealing you in for a load of grief—that's all."

"Thanks," said Frandzen dryly. He wasn't convinced. The wiper was still hanging around waiting for a cue from his boss. Vee turned to me.

"Quit acting like a couple of strange tom-cats in a back alley. You, too. Let's all go up to the Club. I need a drink and we might as well have it there."

I shrugged, said: "Sounds all right to me. But this is Frandzen's party. It's up to him."

He turned his fishy stare in my direction, studied my face for a moment, then nodded.

We went out of there, the wiper bringing up the rear.

WE made the trip down to the *Parfait Club* in uncomfortable silence. But I made up for the lack of talk by doing a lot of heavy thinking. This guy Frandzen was getting in my hair. It was a cinch he was still leery of me—and maybe I was just a little bit more leery of him.

It seemed screwy to me that a lad should get so hot and bothered about his girl. I decided that if he got tough, I'd get tougher.

At the Club we all parked at Frandzen's table. Al made a point of sticking at my side. That muzzler had a one track mind. As a preliminary to the session, Frandzen ordered a bottle of rye. It was a good beginning but before we could go to work on the liquor, Salvy Benetti waddles over to the table.

He jerked his head dramatically at Frandzen, whispered dramatically in his ear. Frandzen scraped back his chair, got up, said: "Stick here—all of you."

I hadn't any other idea. I did the honors with the bottle and just as I was about to drink, Vee Gorman said:

"Why don't you let me come clean with him?"

I put down my glass untasted. I looked hard at her, shook my head in a decided negative.

"Nothing doing, babe," I said. "We'll play this alone."

She flared up. Her mouth hardened and her eyes narrowed. Dagger points of light stabbed out at me.

She said accusingly: "You think he's mixed up in it?"

I shrugged, downed my drink. "I'm putting the finger on no one yet," I said. "On the other hand, I'm counting no one out."

"You're nuts," she shot back, "if you think Eddie was in on that deal."

"Maybe I am." Then I shot one over fast. I said slowly, in a hard voice: "But what if he was?"

She looked at me, saw the death in my eyes, then turned away. "You're making it tough as hell for me," she said sullenly.

"You'll stand up under it," I told her.

And then the little argument was over. Frandzen was headed our way again and tagging along with him was a second gent. They came to a halt by the table and for the first time I saw a crooked half smile on Frandzen's face. I should have known then that something was screwy.

The other lad was short and beefy. He had black eyes, a crooked nose and a loose mouth. He carried a black fedora under the arm of his shiny blue serge suit. He didn't ring true.

Frandzen said: "Here's another gent from Philly, Kilday. Maybe you know him?"

I looked the stranger up and down again, shook my head. "Can't say that I do."

"His name's Dake," said Frandzen. "He's a dick."

I turned and stared at Dake again. I didn't make him. I turned back to Frandzen: "So what?"

Frandzen still had that funny half smile on his face. I had a terrific urge to wipe it off with a straight armed left. He said: "Dake happens to be interested in loogans from Philly. I thought maybe you two could get together."

I sneered, was about to tell Frandzen what I thought of him, then changed my mind. Instead I turned in my chair and looked up at Dake.

"Well, what's the story, copper?" I said.

Dake smiled feebly, revealing a double row of false teeth. "It's too long to tell here," he said. "Maybe some other time."

I wasn't impressed. "Suit yourself," I said. "Do you want me or are you just seeing the sights and collecting faces?"

The smile faded from Dake's lips. His false teeth clicked together. He said in a whining voice: "You look pretty as hell sitting there, Kilday. I wouldn't spoil it."

I said: "Nuts, copper. On your way!"

Dake took out a stick of Wrigley's and stuffed it in his mouth. His false teeth clicked noisily as they worked on the gum. He looked at me for ten-twenty seconds, nodding his head.

"Okay, Kilday," he said at last. "I'll be seeing you later, maybe."

"Sure," I grinned. "I'm at the Bellmore. Drop in some time when I'm out."

CHAPTER VI

Bait

IT happened the next night—late. I was lapping up Martinis in the *Parfait,* mentally kicking myself in the pants for getting no place. And then things began to happen. A slender blonde in a black lace dress, with heavily mascarraed eyes, wafts herself up to my table. The orchestra was playing the *Peanut Vendor.*

The blonde said: "Let's get a load of this struggle—Kilday."

She laid a peculiar emphasis on my name but I didn't know her from Eve.

I said: "Why not," got up from the table and we swung out onto the floor.

I dragged her around the dance oval twice waiting for her to cue. Then I said: "Well, sister, what's the racket?"

She swung me around and I saw her eye up the place. Then she put her chin on my shoulder, her rouged lips close to my ear.

"Joe sent me," she said.

I stiffened slightly. "Yeah?" I said. "So what?"

"Let's go places," she answered, significantly. "Let's get out of here."

I was ready to quit in the middle of the dance and scram. She hung onto me, shook her head slowly from side to side. "Not so fast, big boy. The more quiet we go out of here the better."

The band quit playing and we clapped for an encore. While we waited for the music I said: "What's it all about?"

She said: "Hold it."

The band started playing again and I was burning up as we waltzed. If Joe had sent her, that meant something had broken in Philly. What?

We went out of there, got into a Yellow cab and the blonde gave the driver an address.

In less than twenty minutes the car stopped in front of a smart new apartment house in the upper Seventies. I slipped the driver a bill and we got out.

We went through an ornate lobby, stepped into the automatic elevator, the blonde pressed a button and said: "Not such a bad place."

"I've seen worse," I answered.

The lift stopped at the third floor. We got out of the cage, the kid led the way down the imitation marble corridor and stopped in front of a door lettered 3B.

She fitted a key to the lock, clicked it back, pushed the door open and snapped on the light. I saw a nicely furnished apartment with a real Chinese rug on the floor, a small grand piano, some Japanese prints on the wall, a tasteful sofa and two richly upholstered chairs.

The blonde flung off her wrap, said, "Sit down, Kilday," opened a cupboard, took out glasses and mixed cocktails. We sat down, drank, and then I said:

"Well, babe—Joe sent you. So what?"

She didn't answer me with words. Instead, she squinted at me over the rim of her glass and laughed. I didn't like it. I felt myself getting hot under the collar. I placed my glass carefully on the edge of the table, started to heave myself out of the chair and then she spoke.

She said, still laughing: "Okay, boys, you can come in. This mug is just asking to be taken!"

DIRECTLY opposite me in the center of the far wall were a pair of heavy, velour drapes that masked off the adjoining room. And now those drapes moved, parted before the advance of a pair of glinting automatics.

And the automatics were held in the capable fists of as sweet a pair of wipers as I had ever seen. I gave them a quick once over—low browed, cauliflower eared; a slit for eyes and red gashes where their lips should have been.

I knew the type well; and at the same time knew that my life wasn't worth a plugged nickel.

I turned to the girl, said: "So that's the kind of a louse you are?"

She shrugged, lit a cigarette and flicked the still flaming match straight for my eyes. Then she turned to the wipers.

"Make him squeal for that crack, Manny," she said.

Manny was the beefier of the two torpedoes. He had pig eyes to match his wolf lips. Now he grinned to show fanged, yellow teeth.

"He'll squeal two ways, Lill," he said. "Now scram. This ain't going to be pretty for a lady to see."

Lill pulled her wrap around her, took a final drag on her cigarette and then left. The door closed softly be-

hind her; the key grated ominously in the lock. I eased further back in my chair and grinned as if I liked it.

But not for long. Manny said: "Get up, you!"

I untangled myself from the chair slowly, figuring the odds if I jumped the two guns. Then Manny spoke again.

"Frisk him, Lou."

Lou knew his stuff. It took him just two seconds to unlimber the Luger from my shoulder holster; another five to pat my pockets, hips, thighs and legs, going down.

With two guns boring at me and

my own kicked under the settee, it was a nice spot; a tough spot that was going to take a lot of heavy master-minding to get out of.

That wasn't the only thing I was worried about then. The thing that I had on my mind was this: How did Lill and her boy friends know about Joe? Where was the leak? Who was crossing us—Benetti? Frandzen? Dake? Or all three?

But Manny didn't give me any chance to dope the answer. He hefted the gun in his hand, grinned crookedly and said in a conversational voice:

"Okay, Kilday—where are the plates?"

I had been expecting that. I looked as dumb as a copper.

"What plates, sweetheart?" I asked sweetly.

Manny said: "Horse-feathers, Kilday. The dumb act won't get you nothing. The Pedretti plates—the plates you bumped Lazarus for. Where are they?"

My eyes narrowed suddenly: my jaw stuck out. These mugs knew too much! But it wasn't that that got me. It suddenly struck me like a ton of bricks that these two wipers were the ones who had given the business to Mona.

The thought must have shown in my face; Lou must have read the death in my eye. He stepped forward suddenly, jabbed the nozzle of his gun deep into my navel.

"Don't try it, Kilday!" he clipped from the corner of his mouth. "These walls are sound proof; there isn't another tenant on the floor. One phoney move out of you and I'll blow your ribs out your spine!"

I looked down on him; my lips curled in a sneer.

"Nuts to you, punk," I said. "That isn't your style. You haven't got the guts. You'd sooner work on a broad with cigarette and cigar stubs."

That registered with him and I knew what I wanted. But before I could do anything about it, Lou removed the gun from my navel and placed the nozzle on the bridge of my nose. He slashed it down in a broad swipe. A spurt of blood followed the cold steel. I felt myself boiling, but I held tight.

"You louse!" he said.

I leered at him crookedly, laughed in his teeth.

"So you *were* the rats!" I said bitterly.

Lou stepped back from me. His lips twisted into a snarl and I saw his finger tighten on the trigger. I got ready to stop lead.

Then Manny spoke sharply. "Cut it, Lou! Don't be a horse's rosette. That comes later—if—"

Lou's finger relaxed slowly on the trigger. With a growl he backed up and lined up alongside of Manny.

"I don't like this guy," he said simply.

Manny shook his head. "Neither do I." Then to me: "Get that, Kilday—Lou don't like you and neither do I. That makes it unanimous. You got just about ten seconds to come clean. If you don't, you're going to take the sweetest beating you ever heard about. It's going to be a lot tougher than cigar or cigarette stubs. And it's going to end the same way. You've heard now, Kilday—where are the plates?"

Hot blood was pounding through my brain and all the time I was telling myself to keep my head. Too many things were happening too fast and I had to play them all right. Right then I would have dumped the plates in the Hudson River if I had

had my fist wrapped around the butt of my Luger.

I was willing to pass up the Pedretti plates—willing to take a beating—willing to check out for good, on one condition. And that was, that I took Lou and Manny to hell with me.

My answer must have been too slow in coming for Manny. He said: "Wake him up, Lou!"

Lou grinned, licked a thin stream of saliva off his thin lips. Carefully he shifted his gun to his left hand; carefully he edged up to me from the side so as to keep clear of Manny's gun. I watched him from narrowed eyes. My head and shoulders began to weave from side to side. Lou's right hand knotted into a hard fist, his muscles bulged. Then his arm shot forward.

He crossed me. Instead of aiming for the head, his fist landed like a jolt of dynamite above my heart. I doubled up and then Lou crossed me again. His foot shot out and the point of his number 10D sank six inches into the pit of my stomach.

I fought the cloud of blackness that was battling the shooting flames in my brain. My heart suddenly swelled up and I thought it would explode under my ribs. I felt bleeding inside and there was the salty taste of blood in my mouth.

I went down slowly to the floor, joint by joint, braced myself by stiff forearms. For ten seconds, maybe, I studied the intricate pattern of the carpet. Then I crawled up again.

I was as helpless as a babe. That kick to the stomach had paralyzed me. Manny must have known it, for he lowered his gun and studied my face with a wolfish interest. Lou's lips were slobbering.

Manny said: "Lou gets a hell of a lot of fun kicking mugs like you. He's peculiar that way. Next time he'll kick lower! Better come clean, Kilday!"

It took all the strength I had to say: "Damn you! Both of you!"

Manny said: "You're asking for it and you're going to get it. This is just the prelims." Then he gave the nod to Lou.

That gent dropped his gun into his pocket and with a calculating eye, measured me from head to foot. I still couldn't raise my hands above my hips.

Then he stepped in close. His right blasted off my chin, snapped my head back. My knees buckled and as I sagged forward he grabbed me by the slack of my coat, straightened me out again with a second stiff armed right to the button. A bomb exploded in my brain.

Lou dusted me off, let me fall. I flattened my nose on the carpet and where I lay a little pool of blood gathered round my head.

Lou cheated on the bell. Five seconds later he kicked me back to life again with his boot in my ribs. He yanked me to my feet, propped me against the wall.

"You're not so tough, bright boy!"

He never gave me a chance for a come-back. He brought his knee up and crossed with his left.

"I'll soften you—you heel!"

He broke the knuckle of his right fist on my jaw; fractured the ribs around my heart with his left.

My guts were tangled into a hard knot; my stomach was heaving. A hot needle stabbed my heart every time I drew breath.

Lou knew his stuff and took a pride in his work. I took a concentrated beating for three minutes propped against the wall; another minute of it with my face in the carpet as he gave me the boot. It might have been longer but I passed out then.

Manny slopped a shot of gin into my battered face. The liquid ate like hot acid into my pulped flesh. I kicked a leg, crawled to hands and knees, swayed there, unable to climb to my feet.

Lou placed his shoe on the back of my neck.

"How about it, tough guy?" he asked hopefully.

I gave him the answer he was hoping for. I said:

"Damn you—you rat!"

He threw his weight on the foot he had on the nape of my neck. My nose flattened itself against the floor. He rubbed it in to my eyes, to my mouth until I gagged on the nap of the carpet. I would have still been there if the other hadn't called him off.

Manny yanked me to my feet, held my collapsed body upright by my neck-tie till I thought the hangman's noose was around my wind-pipe. He placed the nozzle of his automatic under the tip of my nose. His eyes were yellow with hate, his lips worked and twin spots of color flamed in his ashen cheeks.

Lou was happy to beat me up. Manny would have been happier to plug me.

He said:

"God damn you, Kilday—talk—or take it!"

I couldn't talk if I had wanted to. My face was blue from the neck-tie around my throat. My lungs threatened to explode or collapse, I don't know which. The only faculty I had left was my eyes and they were glued to Manny's eyes. I saw them narrow to pin-points; knew before he did when his brain sent the impulse to his finger to constrict on the trigger.

His voice was hoarse and cracked and sudden beads of sweat popped out on his forehead.

"You asked for it!" he panted. "Now—"

I didn't hear the shot of the gun. All I was aware of was that Manny's narrowed eyes flew wide. A dumb, surprised look came over his face. His grip relaxed on my neck-tie. His automatic came down from my nose, slowly as if it was too heavy for him.

Then he toppled forward taking me with him.

As I went down three things registered on my fogged brain. Lou whirled, crouched and whipped up his gun. From the neighborhood of the door I heard a sharp crack. Then the automatic was sailing out of Lou's hand and he was going after it in a nose dive.

That was all for a long time. I came to gagging over a shot of Scotch. It seemed an hour before I could force open my eyes. Then I blinked up into the cadaverous face of Detective Dake—Dake who had bumped both Manny and Lou just when they were going to give me the business!

I was too groggy to figure that one out!

Dake said wryly with a twisted grin: "You can take it, all right. But I don't know why in the hell I saved you. You're no use to anybody now."

I never had liked Dake and I didn't like him then. But he had yanked me off the hottest spot of my career and I grinned at him appreciatingly.

"How did you get here?" I mumbled from puffed lips.

Dake took out a stick of Wrigley's and clamped his false teeth around it. He chewed noisily for ten seconds before answering. Then:

"Followed you!"

"Yeah? Too bad you didn't bust it up a little sooner," I said nastily.

He clicked his plate together two or three times absent-mindedly, sucked in on the gum and made a sharp, popping noise. He grinned as if he was pleased with his act.

"Did you ever stop to figure, Kilday," he said slowly, "that maybe I'm just as interested in the Pedretti plates as those two chiselers?"

He held the bottle to my lips. I took a long swallow, felt it down to my heels. Then I crawled to my hands and feet and dragged myself into a chair. I ached all over. My head felt like a balloon, my eyes were puffed and closed and my lower jaw unhinged.

My heart felt like it was trying to lift a piano as it hammered against a pair of busted ribs. I tried another shot from the bottle. I had to have something to go on. I looked from the bodies of Manny and Lou draped on the floor up into Dake's hollow face.

I was beginning to respect that guy. I said:

"About the Pedretti plates—so what?"

Dake tried grin at me. His upper plate fell away from the roof of his mouth, revealing a row of shrunken, blue gums.

"Lou was a damned sight better at beating you up than I would ever be. Let it ride for a while."

"Swell by me," I said.

"Can you travel?"

"As far as a cab."

"Oke. Stick here a minute."

Dake went out. I had lied to him. I could travel a damn sight farther than to a cab. As soon as the door had closed behind him, I dropped to my hands and knees. I sweated blood but I crawled across that floor to the settee on the far side, fished out my Luger and crawled back again. Three minutes later when Dake returned I was slumped in the chair again.

CHAPTER VII

Vee Points a Finger

THE sawbones did a pretty good job on me. Two days later I was around and going places. And most of them were the *Parfait Club.*

Even though I was pretty sure that Manny and Lou were the two gorillas who had given the business to Mona, I was a damn sight more sure that they were working under orders from some one higher up. And the more I butted into things the hotter became Frandzen's night club.

But this last play of Dake's was screwy as hell. Vee Gorman thought so, too. I met her a couple of nights later in the foyer of the club, just as I was about to surrender the fedora to the check-room blonde. We sat down on a bench near the telephone booths.

"I heard there was a party," she said. "Tell me."

I told her. That is, I told her almost everything. When I got to Dake and the good Samaritan act, her eyebrows met in a frown. She shook her head.

"Funny. I don't make it at all," she said. "Something smells."

I lit a cigarette, inhaled slowly, said:

"You're telling me? I don't figure Dake for any boy scout either." I looked at her hard, then turned away. Then I went on. "But the funny thing, kid, the smell keeps coming back to the Club, here. What do you make of that?"

If she made anything of it at all,

I didn't hear just then. The drapes that screened off the Club proper parted and Salvy Benetti pushed his fat bulk in our direction. His little blue eyes were lost in rolls of fat as he grinned at the girl. He shoved an envelope into my hand.

"From Philly," he said significantly.

I mumbled a "Thanks"; Benetti made one or two cracks to the kid, then waddled back to the Club again. I studied the envelope briefly, recognized the handwriting. As I thrust a thumb under the flap, Vee got up. I grasped her arm and pulled her back again.

"Stick around. It's from Joe. Maybe something's broke."

I shook out the single sheet of cheap note paper. The message was brief—too brief. It left me wondering plenty. I read:

> Dear Pete:
> Frandzen's joint too hot for me. By the time you get this will be in New York. Under cover at 1064 West Charlton. 5D. Ring three times. Make it as soon as you get this.
> Joe.

I read it through twice, passed it over to the girl.

"Something's popping. Joe don't scare easy."

She read the brief lines, handed the message back to me.

"I got the heap at the curb. I'll drive you over."

We got going. I liked that girl. No wasted words; no lost motion. She'd come through in a pinch.

She said nothing more until we turned into Charlton. Then, without turning her head: "I'll drop you off at the corner. Then I'll park the bus opposite the place and keep the engine going. Oke?"

I hopped out when she slowed down at the intersection, went the rest of the way on foot. It was late and the street was practically deserted. I found number 1064 on a grimy transom. It was a six story apartment house that had seen better days. A gloomy warehouse flanked it on one side and a narrow alley on the other. I mounted the steps, saw the roadster swing into the block and then felt the door knob turn under my fingers.

It was a walk-up. I climbed the five flights of stairs with their fraying carpet. The corridor on the fifth floor was like all the others—dimly-lit and quiet. Just to be on the safe side I kept my right hand buried in my pocket, wrapped around the Luger while I hunted for 5D.

I found the right door. I found the bell push beside the panel and jammed my left thumb on the buzzer.

One—two—

Inside the bell pealed shrilly. Then a dull *plop* exploded behind the door and drowned it out.

Joe had said—ring three times. I laughed like hell! Someone had punched the bell the third time for me—and with a silenced gat!

I jumped back. Then I hit that door with my shoulders. Wood screeched, splintered beneath the impact. I hit it again and on the third lunge the lock gave. The door banged back and I pitched into the room. My arms flailed the air as I tried to regain my balance, failed and landed on my knees beside the body of Joe Bassett.

The brilliant flood of light from the fixture overhead told the story. I looked at the widening circle of crimson between his shoulder blades. Then I climbed to my feet and made for the open window across the room. I stuck my head out.

It was a dumb stunt. God knows why I wasn't blasted. Anyway, I got nothing for my pains—not even a dose of lead. A fire escape led

downwards but it was black as the Pit in that alley. I couldn't see the rungs of the ladder after they passed the third floor.

I went back to Joe, straddled his body and looked down at it for a long minute. Things were beginning to click in my mind. Then I knelt down, rolled the body over. Joe was dead! Very dead.

I cursed viciously. Joe was no saint but he was a square shooter. Now he was gone. Again I cursed the yellow rat who had plugged him; then I called myself a damn fool. Crying over Joe wouldn't bring him back and it was time I got down to business.

I began a hasty but thorough search through his pockets. The other plate. Joe had probably brought it with him from Philly.

But I didn't find it. I didn't expect to. Joe hadn't been killed just to give the undertaker some work.

I straightened up, looked the room over. His bag was on a chair in the corner.

I was rooting through a litter of clothing when a voice sounded from the doorway behind me.

"That's swell, Kilday. Hold it!"

There was a *plop*. No, not a silenced gun, this time. Just the sound of chewing gum masticated by a set of phoney ivories.

I kept my hands extended before me, slowly pivoted around and stared into Dake's cadaverous face. He favored me with a fanged grin, batted one eye at the body of Joe lying at my feet.

"Not so hot," he said. "What have you got to say for yourself, Kilday?"

The muzzle of the gun in his fist gaped hungrily at my belt buckle. I looked down the long barrel and decided that I had nothing to say.

He stepped up closer, jerked the gun casually to indicate the body sprawled between us.

"This is just what I been waiting for," he said conversationally. "You got away with the Lazarus job but this one will do just as well. You can only fry a guy once, anyway."

I shook my head. "Wrong again, Dake. My Luger never did this job. It hasn't been fired. And when the saw-bones digs the bullet out of Joe, that'll cinch it."

He grinned again—a nasty, blue-gummed grimace.

"Got it all pat, eh?" he sneered. "But it won't stick. Of course you wouldn't use your own cannon. You used another gun for the job, then sailed it out the window." He smacked his gum with great relish and looked pleased as hell. "No, Kilday, this time you're *It!* Are you going to make a fuss or do I have to . . . ?"

He raised his automatic suggestively. I went into a frantic mastermind. The idea of trailing meekly along was out—I didn't even consider it. I might just as well have climbed into the chair and begged the executioner to throw the switch.

What then?

I had just about decided to jump his rod and take the million to one gamble he'd miss, when an angel suddenly materialized in the doorway. At least she looked like an angel to me just then.

"Your turn, Dake," came Vee Gorman's calm voice. "Drop the gat and look at this one!"

He didn't follow her instructions exactly. He leaped to one side and flashed a quick glance over his shoulder at the same time. But I knew a break when I saw one.

The point of my shoe caught him in the wrist and knocked his aim all to hell. His gun roared, chipped plaster and dust from the far wall.

The gun sailed from his fingers and as he dove for it, I straightened him up with a short armed left. Then I hit him as hard as I could on the point of the jaw with my right.

I heard his bridge work crumple. A shower of false teeth spewed from his mouth. His eyes rolled back in their sockets until only the whites showed. Then his knees buckled and he smacked the floor beside Joe.

I turned to Vee Gorman. What a kid! She had pulled her little act with nothing more deadly about her than her finger nail.

I told her all the nice things and then we got away from there.

CHAPTER VIII

Benetti Gets Dealt In

THE kid dropped me off a block away from the *Parfait Club.* I figured on fireworks and I didn't think it wise to have her tagging along. Anyway, she had done her good deed for one day.

Swell kid—Vee Gorman.

My Luger was handy in the side pocket of my coat as I walked through the gaudy entrance of Frandzen's joint. The doorman gave me a big grin as if I was the prize butter and egger along the main stem. Nothing suspicious there.

Inside the Club I gave the place a quick once over. Crowded as usual, but Frandzen's table was deserted and there was no sign of him or Benetti on the floor.

All to the good.

All the lights were dark save a couple of baby spots that were playing up the legs of the handful of undressed blondes doing their stuff on the dance floor. Under cover of the darkness I made a bee-line for the door to my right marked private.

It was too dark for me to read the sign. I went right on through.

Salvy Benetti looked up from his desk on my entrance. He waved a fat, diamond studded hand vaguely through the air in welcome. His fat face broke into a smile.

But I didn't answer it. I said in a hard voice:

"This is the kiss-off, fat-face."

His little blue eyes searched mine with a puzzled expression. Then they dropped to my coat pocket, saw the bulging outline of the Luger beneath the cloth. His eyes narrowed, his nostrils dilated and I saw a pulse begin to hammer in his throat.

He looked up at me warily, shook his head from side to side.

"I don't get you," he said.

"No?" I flung back. "Maybe you get this. Joe's dead!"

"Joe?" he echoed.

I laughed in his face. "It's a nice routine, Benetti. But it leaves me cold. Joe's not only dead—he was spotted! And you're the rat who put the works to him!"

He went white. His thin, straw color hair seemed to stand up on end.

"You're nuts," he said in a choked voice.

And then I saw his pudgy hand sneak across the desk top to a row of buttons. I unlimbered the Luger and punched it under his nose.

"Press that button and you'll wake up in hell."

Benetti's hand froze where it was. He looked up at me, through me and beyond me. He had forgotten about the button, forgotten about my Luger. His eyes squinted.

He mumbled, more to himself than to me: "So, Joe's dead, eh?" Then he looked straight at me again. The cold steel of my gun sticking under his nose didn't bother him at all. His voice was hard and despite his fat jowls his face was hard. For the first time Benetti looked like a killer—a tough gunman and killer.

He said: "You're screwy as hell, Kilday! What makes you think I spotted Joe?"

"That letter. It made an appointment with me. You opened it!"

He shook his head, looked straight down the barrel of the Luger, said:

"Why would I want to bump Joe?"

I wasn't impressed. I said: "That one's easy."

"He did me a big favor once. I owed him a lot."

"And you paid it with lead!"

A hot wave of color started from the top of Benetti's collar and traveled up his fat neck. Little flecks of red showed in the pale irises of his blue eyes. His upper lip pulled up under his nose in a snarl.

He had a lot of nasty things on his mind, but before he could say them a voice said behind me—Frandzen's frozen voice:

"Drop the gat, Kilday!"

I stiffened but I didn't drop the gat. And even though I didn't turn around I knew that Frandzen was standing in the doorway, an automatic in his fist.

His voice came again, sharp and cold.

"Drop it!"

"This rat spotted a pal of mine," I said.

Frandzen wasn't interested in the details. He said:

"I don't give a damn who he spotted! You can't come into my Club and get away with gun-play."

"The hell I can't!" I growled.

I ducked, side-stepped fast, dropped to one knee and pivoted behind Benetti's chair.

Frandzen's automatic boomed twice, very rapidly. Benetti's eyes bugged out as long slivers from his desk top splashed up into his face. He froze to his chair, arms stretched out before him, never moving a muscle.

Outside on the floor of the Club, the jazz band was blasting away at *Nickel in the Slot*. So far, the brass had drowned out the noise of our little private party. But it couldn't last long.

Frandzen cursed bitterly. His frozen face had melted at last. He lunged away from the door, moved fast along the wall.

I poked out my fedora from behind Benetti's beefy shoulders. Frandzen squeezed lead and I felt the hat jerk in my hand.

Pretty good shooting, that—but not good enough!

The Luger talked—just once—and settled the argument. Frandzen cursed bitterly, watched his automatic sail from his shattered fist, arch towards the ceiling, then clatter to the floor in the far corner.

Outside, the band had stopped playing. When I got to my feet I was full of ideas. I backed carefully to the door, keeping both Frandzen and

Benetti under the point of my gun.

"I'm going places, gents," I said. "I'll be seeing you both later."

CHAPTER IX

Boomerang Double-Cross

THERE was a fleet of cabs lined up at the curb outside the *Parfait Club.* I slipped to the outside of the first one on the line. The hackie, a big bruiser, was sitting behind the wheel reading a tab sheet.

I grinned, waved a ten-spot before his Semitic nose.

"It's real," I said.

"Sure it is," he answered, giving me the eye. "What do I got to do—murder?"

That mug wasn't dumb—no New York cab driver is. We understood each other perfectly.

I said: "Listen. I got a hunch a big fat guy is going to come out of the Club any minute now. Maybe you know him—Benetti?"

He nodded his head.

"He's going to grab your cab. The ten spot is yours if I can park here on the running board and find out where he's going. That's your job. You're hard of hearing, see? Make him repeat the address twice—and loud."

The hackman grinned a jagged-tooth grin. His greasy hand went out for the ten spot.

"Bag, brother," he said. "Get out of sight."

I ducked low on the running board and not too soon. Seconds later I heard heavy feet pound across the sidewalk, heard the door of the cab swing open.

My driver knew his stuff. With a professional flourish he snapped down the flag on his meter. Then I heard his thick voice.

"Where to, bud?"

I hung on the answer, had to make sure of two things. First, that it was Benetti in the bus; second, if it was he, his destination.

It was Benetti, all right.

"Borden Hotel," he said. "And make it fast."

The driver earned the ten spot. He repeated: "Borden Hotel? That's on Twenty-seventh Street, ain't it?"

Benetti's bass rumbled out impatiently.

"Yeah—just off Madison. Get going."

The cab got under way and I slid off the running board. Two minutes later I was leaning back on the cushions of another headed for the same joint.

Benetti's cab was just pulling away from the curb before the Borden Hotel when mine turned into Twenty-seventh Street. But he was nowhere in sight. I paid off my bus, flicked my cigarette into the gutter and strolled into the hotel.

It was a cheap joint—a house of call—one of those places where all the names on the register are "Mr. John Smith and wife."

The dapper, gray-haired gent behind the desk operated the switchboard and the solitary elevator. Handling the job he did, in a house like the Borden, I figured him to be plenty wise.

There was no one else in the lobby. I gave him the nod and we stepped into the elevator cage. He looked at me shrewdly. I flashed a double saw buck, this time.

"A fat faced gent just came in here," I said. "What room?"

He looked at me for a long ten seconds, then down at the twenty. He shrugged.

"305."

"Fourth floor," I said, slipping him the bill.

He banged the door of the cage and we shot up. I stopped him before he

could open the door on the fourth floor. In my left hand I held a C note; in my right—the Luger.

I said: "How about a pass key?"

He cocked one eye at the gun and shied off.

"Christ, fella," he said, "I'm willing to oblige but I don't want to get into a jam."

"You don't know anything, see? I must have slipped up the stairs when you took fat-face up in the elevator. I want that pass key. You're going to collect for it one way or another. What's it going to be? The C note or do I rap this gat over your head?"

He shrugged again. "You win, mister. But, Christ, keep me out of it. I got in a jam once and it was plenty."

He fished out a key from his pocket and slipped it to me. I told him he had nothing to worry about, just to attend to his knitting. He opened the elevator door and I got out.

I waited until the car had dropped down to the lobby, then I took the stairs to the floor below.

There were four dark corridors leading away from the elevator shaft and on the third try I located the one that led to 305. I tip-toed to the door. But I didn't have to put my ear to the panel.

The angry buzz of two voices came out to me. I recognized them both—Benetti's and another. They were talking about me, about Joe—about the Pedretti plates. And they were both sore as hell!

I didn't wait for any more. I slipped the key into the lock, had it half turned when a voice rang out from the room, sharp with panic.

"Don't—don't—for Christ sake don't . . ."

A dull explosion punctuated the words. Then there was a cough breaking on a bubble of blood, followed by a thud as a body hit the floor.

I didn't give a damn if every copper in the precinct was charging down on the Borden Hotel. I went in that room, closed and locked the door behind me.

Dake was lying on the floor, his sightless eyes staring at the ceiling. His mouth sagged open wide. His false teeth were gone and only his blue, shrunken gums showed. A thin trickle of blood was oozing out of a hole in his neck.

And bending over him, gun in one hand, one of the Pedretti plates in the other, was Salvy Benetti.

I let him have it.

I WALKED into the lobby of the *Parfait Club* and literally bumped into Frandzen. And for the second time that night, that frigid gent was shocked out of his stony calm. He glared at me and a hot wave of color crept slowly up over his stony features.

"You—damn you! Where's Benetti?"

"In hell, probably," I told him wearily.

His huge body jerked as though a bullet had struck him. Then his right arm crooked suggestively. I looked my disgust.

"Keep your shirt on," I advised him. "He wasn't worth it. Where's Vee? I'm ready to talk and she'll want to be in on the story."

For a minute he still looked murder. Then at last he shrugged. "I'll listen, Kilday. But it better be good."

"It is," I said.

He turned abruptly and led the way inside. A few minutes later we were seated at his table and Vee joined us. She looked at me questioningly. I gave her the nod and a low sigh of relief escaped her. I turned, talked to Frandzen but I knew the kid was hanging on my words.

"It begins in Philly," I started. "Me and a rat named Joe Bassett pulled the Lazarus job—copped the Pedretti plates."

Frandzen looked hard at me.

"Well—why not?" I said.

Frandzen didn't answer. Instead he reached for the bottle, poured a stiff four fingers, downed it.

"Go on," he said. "I'm listening."

That guy had a heart of stone to go along with his frozen face. I lit up a cigarette, took a deep inhale. After all, to hell with Frandzen. He meant nothing to me. I had squared things with Mona. Five rats were behind her killing—and those five rats were frying in hell!

Vee Gorman must have read the thought on my face. She dropped her cool fingers on my hot ones.

"Go on," she said. "I want to hear."

I shrugged, said, "Sure," turned back to Frandzen.

"After the job Bassett and I split the plates between us—just to make sure. A damn good thing we did. We decided to lay low till the stink blew over. We were sitting pretty and there was no use spoiling things by forcing our luck."

It was my turn to take a shot from the bottle. Then my lips curled bitterly with the memory.

"Did I say we were sitting pretty? That shows how screwy I was. While I was smoking butts and drinking bad booze waiting for the cops to drop the Lazarus case, my pal—good old Joe Bassett—sold me down the river. One plate wasn't enough for him.

"He figured I had given my plate to my girl for safekeeping. He crossed me—sold me out to Benetti and Dake. That dick stuff had me fooled for a while. But Dake was no more than a yellow rat who couldn't take it when his number was up."

I broke off abruptly, eyed Frandzen across the table.

"Like it so far?"

"It listens swell," he said. "I'll save the questions till you're finished. Go on."

I oiled my tongue with another shot of Scotch.

"Benetti and Dake send a pair of wipers to Philly to work out on Mona. They work out on her plenty and draw a blank. The poor kid didn't know where I had the plate." My voice hardened. "Then they bumped her!"

Frandzen said: "Tough; but where do I and the kid fit in?"

"I'm coming to that. Alongside of Mona's body was a packet of matches—a packet of matches from this Club here. That brought me to New York on the run. And then the fun began!"

Frandzen nodded sourly. "You're telling me?" he said bitterly.

"I am," I shot back. And I told him—told him all the story—the details he knew—and those he didn't. He listened, all right, and liked it.

I began the tale with gun play and I ended it that way. But when I was finished there was a puzzled frown on both Frandzen's and the girl's face. There was silence for a moment while they thought it over. Then the girl spoke.

"But if Dake was in on the deal, why did he kill Manny and Lou when they were giving you the business?"

I smiled, felt my fractured ribs.

"Because they *were* giving me the business," I answered. "The whole works. If Dake hadn't bumped them, they would have bumped me. And that was the last thing Dake wanted, then. Those two wipers didn't mean anything to him—but *I* did—till he got my plate. If Manny had bumped me, Dake's play was shot to hell! Got it?"

Vee nodded and looked at Frandzen. Frozen face was toying with his whiskey glass, looking out into space. Suddenly he shot one over.

"What about this hole? Who killed Bassett—and why?"

I was expecting it. I shot it right back to him.

"That's easy. That letter from Bassett that Benetti delivered to me was a frame. It was to put me on the spot. But by this time Dake was getting hoggish. He thought he saw a way of out master-minding both Bassett and Benetti. He beat me to the Charlton Street address, bumped Bassett, lifted his plate from him and then pulled the copper stuff on me. Would have gotten away with it, too, if it hadn't been for Vee.

"He had Bassett's plate. All he had to do was to get mine and he was bagged!"

Frandzen drummed his fingers on the table top for a moment. He started to ask a question, then changed his mind. Instead he said: "Go on."

I went on.

"After Vee pulled the rescue act I came back to the Club here. I was still in a fog. I hadn't tumbled yet. I accused Benetti of putting Joe on the spot.

"Of course, he hadn't but he tumbled to Dake's play and when he did, he acted so damn queer that I tumbled, too. The rest is a cinch.

"When Benetti scrammed out of the Club I followed him. And as I expected, he led me straight to Dake's hide-out. From there on it was dog eat dog. And I happened to be the last dog on the scene!"

I paused, looked hard at Frandzen.

"Good enough?" I asked.

He nodded slowly. "It'll get by in a pinch, but where in the hell does Vee fit in the picture?"

"Vee? Oh, I forgot to mention it. Vee and Mona were sisters."

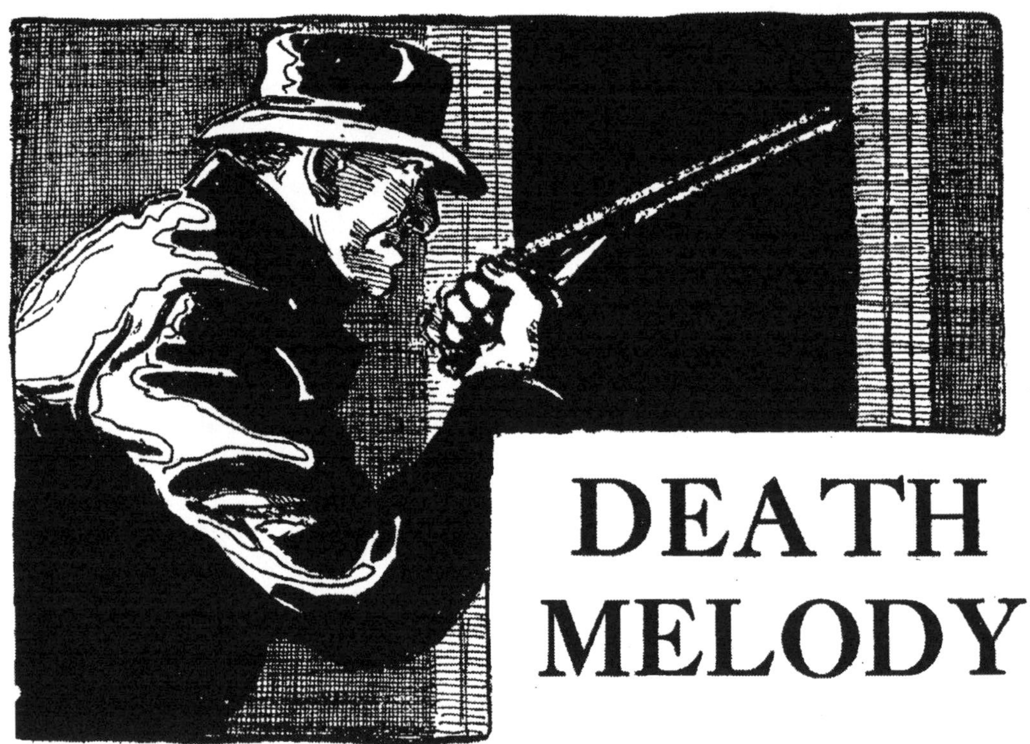

DEATH MELODY

By MARTIN FRANCIS

LOW-TONED organ music surged through the ornate country home on the wooded hill. It quavered, it gurgled, it beat with increasing crescendo against the ears of Knifer Wheeland and Alonzo De Ricco. They sat stiffly in upholstered chairs in Louie Campolo's first-floor bedroom watching their wounded chief battle death, and wondered who would take his place. Outside, gray dusk diffused the blood red of the sun with dull purple; the wind quieted; through the open windows of the sick man's room drifted the heavy fragrance of lilacs, the lonely croaking of frogs in the creek by the road.

Louie's black shaggy head moved, and his dark, sunken eyes solemnly regarded his two lieutenants. The black bristles of the gang chief's beard dotted his pallid flesh like oil-soaked pin pricks in a white sheet.

"I—I'm dyin', boys, dyin'!" he gasped through thick lips. "One of you's got to head the gang when I'm gone. Th—there's an envelope in my safe—" He paused and his eyes took on a dreamy ecstatic expression as the organ music lifted to a mighty roar. "Ain't that music swell, boys? Eighty grand that organ cost me—eighty grand."

"Yeah!" Knifer Wheeland bent forward, his lean bony face aglow with interest. "You said yer had an envelope?" His voice was soft with desire.

A frown creased Louie Campolo's broad white forehead. Tiny beads of perspiration appeared on the long ridges of flesh as his lips twisted. Bart Magliconi's bullet, still lodged in his ribs, was a constant torture.

"Yeah, I got an envelope in the safe. Four—four days after I die, you boys get the gang up here and open the safe. F-four days—not a day sooner. Then you'll know who I want to be leader." His glance swept the burly De Ricco and the lean Wheeland. "All my swag's in a safety deposit vault at the First National. There's $200,000 in cash. The new leader gets $100,000 and the rest I want split between the boys —even, get me?"

De Ricco and Wheeland gasped. Two hundred grand was a lot of money—to split.

Louie's eyes dimmed then centered on the young sleek-haired organist in the next room visible through the French doors. His lips moved as he summoned his fast ebbing strength in another effort to speak.

"M-Mike!" he called. "Throw her up there!" With a wave of his hand he indicated a distant balcony.

Instantly the music flowed from hidden pipes near the high ceiling, and Campolo closed his eyes in ecstasy. Several moments passed. Wheeland and De Ricco exchanged puzzled glances. Louie's eyes opened once more. They were filmy with death.

"Th—throw her down in the basement, Mike!" he ordered weakly, his lips tight with pain. "In the basement."

The music in the balcony died away. There was a pause, then a low rumbling sound issued from below, under the bedroom, and the muffled music drifted upward through the floor. Louie Campolo tried to rise on his elbow, his lined faced wreathed with a wan smile.

"Swell music, eh guys?" he managed to ask proudly. "Y-you know I ain't a tough mugg wid no love for the swell things. Not me. I'm high class. Cripes, it makes me feel good. And when I'm gone the guy what takes my place can have the organ, too. But remember, wait'll four days after I'm dead before you open the safe. That's all I'm askin'. I don't want either of you to git hoggish." His glassy eyes fixed upon De Ricco and Wheeland as though he sought to read their minds. "Y-you're the only two muggs what know the combination of the safe," he went on haltingly. "If you open it before time, I got somethin' that'll guard the interest of the rest of the boys and—" Louie choked and his waxlike face became congested with a dull red.

De Ricco and Wheeland exchanged glances again like two tigers silently measuring strength. Each sought to know the other's thoughts; each tried to mask the question that lay uppermost in their minds: "Am I the man?"

Again Louie Campolo began to cough violently. His heavy hand clasped his breast as if he would ease a pain. A bright liquid red stained the white of the bed sheets, then Louie sank inert on the bed with the mournful throbbing of the organ in his lifeless ears.

Knifer Wheeland was lost in gloomy thought as he sat in Slugger Mott's Cafe munching a hamburger in late afternoon after Louie Campolo's funeral. Two long days yet before Louie's safe could be opened and the important envelope brought forth. Was he or De Ricco the new leader? The uncertainty tortured Knifer.

Jealousy ate at his heart. De Ricco and Louie had been rather chummy of late. That might mean something. Knifer's long fingers clenched, and his eyes narrowed. Damn Louie's soul if he hadn't rewarded him after all these years of service.

Could it be that Louie knew he had held out on him for the past three years, filching an extra share of the loot before Louie had checked it in? No, Louie was dumb in lots of ways.

A thought like a maggot crawled to realization in Knifer's crafty brain. Why not open Louie's safe tonight and learn in advance who the new leader would be? Perhaps there was some extra cash in the safe, too, which he wouldn't have to share with the rest of the gang.

His blood aflame with excitement, Knifer snapped his cigarette to the floor and left the greasy confines of Slugger Mott's establishment. He hailed a taxi and directed the driver to the outskirts of Louie's spacious country estate. Dismissing the man a half mile from the grounds, Knifer cut through the cool hardwoods and slowly approached the big house, clearly visible in the moonlight of the soft May night.

There was a light in the kitchen. Knifer surmised that Gunner Andrews, a crippled gorilla who was Louie's trusted watchman, was perhaps making a cup of coffee for his supper. Knifer knew the location of every window and door in the house. One living room window had a weak latch. Knifer had noticed that the day De Ricco and he had visited the dying Louie.

He moved noiselessly to the window. From his belt he pulled forth a long dagger and inserted its edge under the hard wood. He applied pressure, and, with a slight rasping sound the window moved upward.

Five minutes later Knifer was at the safe. His long, tense fingers played at the dial with experienced touch. As he worked, his teeth were bared in a wolfish snarl. He felt a deep-rooted resentment against his dead chief. Louie knew he was the logical man to head the gang. Why had he held out on him this way?

He completed the combination and rubbed his palms on his trousers in joyous anticipation. Hold out on him, eh? Well, if De Ricco's name was on that envelope, he'd tear it up. They'd never chisel him that way.

With tense fingers Knifer grasped the handle of the safe and yanked. All he ever heard was a slight click. Then came a blinding flash that tore consciousness and life from him.

Gunner Andrews, rushing in from the kitchen after the explosion, found part of an envelope and a four-day time bomb lying amid the débris on the floor. Louie Campolo's handwriting was visible in one corner; therefore Gunner picked up the envelope. A torn photo, streaked with powder, slipped from the ragged edges and fell face downward on the rug. Across the back of the photo was written, "Your new leader if—"

The picture was torn off there so Gunner could only surmise the rest. He turned the photo over and looked at it. A thin tapering face with sharp cruel eyes met his gaze—the face of Knifer Wheeland!

LEAD AND LYRICS

By ANATOLE FELDMAN

CHAPTER I

The Set-up

THE Royale Hotel did its best to live up to its name. It was a resplendent, gingerbread affair with much polished marble and onyx. There were costly oriental rugs on the floors, heavy velour drapes hung in the doorways—and the place was lousy with gaudy uniformed, gold-braided flunkeys.

It was definitely the policy of the Royale to frown on poverty. From the manager down to the lowliest doorman, the help had been trained to turn up a supercilious nose at any one who didn't smack of the Gold Coast.

And Red McGuire didn't smack of the Gold Coast. As a matter of fact, along with a raft of other young McGuires (black Irish fighting stock) he originated in the Stockyards Ward—the Bloody Fourth.

All of which, if the head doorman at the Royale had known he might have acted differently. But he didn't know. So when young McGuire swaggered up to the main door of the hotel, all he saw was a ragged, dirty-faced kid. The seat of the urchin's pants was out, there were no knees to his stockings, and the thatch of red hair that escaped from beneath his grimy hat was a rakish halo to his reckless blue eyes.

"Scram, kid," said the flunkey in accents as haughty as the word permitted.

But Mr. McGuire didn't scram. He had to see a guy—a guy in that hotel. He was going places and he was in a hurry. No mug in a uniform and brass buttons was going to stop him. Mr. McGuire entertained a great scorn and disdain for any uniform.

He kept right on going for the door. The doorman should have known better again; but he didn't. He made a heavy handed lunge for McGuire. McGuire hadn't dodged taxis in the Bloody Fourth for nothing. He side-stepped adroitly and with the speed, finesse, and accuracy that only a gutter-snipe can display, kicked the flunkey smartly in the shins.

He got through the revolving door without further trouble.

In the lobby he side-stepped a frowning porter, thumbed his pug nose inelegantly at the bell captain, tripped over an indignant matron's train and skidded down a long stretch of polished marble straight for the bar of the hostelry.

But here he met with disaster. His advance was abruptly checked by the heavy hand of Grogan, the house dick.

"Get out," growled Mr. Grogan.

"Lay off. I got to see a guy," protested McGuire.

"Beat it, kid," rumbled Grogan heavily.

"But I tell you this is important, see. You house dicks are too big for your jobs. Take your hand off me. I gotta. . . ."

The little session was creating quite a scene A ring of amused spectators hemmed in the kid and the detective. Some one laughed and Mr. Grogan lost his temper. He made the fatal error of pushing Mr. McGuire. Mr. McGuire recoiled backward, recovered, squared off and started his rush forward.

And it was at this psychological moment that a towering mountain of a man loomed in the doorway leading to the bar. His ears were misshapen—long since cauliflowered by a score of men who were artists at their job. His eyes were wild and reckless, his mobile mouth as sensitive as a woman's. And between these two features an enormous, Gargantuan nose pulsed and glowed with a fierce energy.

"Big Nose" Serrano!

And behind him, blocked by his massive width of shoulder, stood his never failing ally through hell or high water—the dour-faced, saturnine Charlie LeBrett.

Now, with a frowning disapproval, his massive head cocked judiciously to one side, Big Nose watched young McGuire square away at the burly Grogan.

"The kid's good," he said in an aside to LeBrett. Then he exploded. "Lead with your left, Red—lead with your left!" He lumbered forward across the lobby. "How many times do I got to tell you never to lead with your right?"

Young McGuire looked up at him sheepishly. "I was outweighed here, so I thought I'd change me style," he offered.

Serrano ran the back of a hard fist

across his nose. "Yeah?" he said skeptically. "Well, don't. Now watch. See—here's how it's done."

Abruptly, he threw up his hands, sank his head between his shoulders. He confronted Grogan.

"Listen, mug, when a pal of mine comes to the hotel, I want to see him. Get it?"

Grogan nodded sulkily.

"Swell," rumbled Serrano. "Now get this!"

Swiftly he feinted with his right, crossed a neat left to Grogan's chin. Dempsey couldn't have done it more cleanly. It was a mere love tap but Grogan staggered wildly back, pawing futilely at the air for balance.

Big Nose felt better after that. With a pleased, childish smile on his lips and his bulbous nose radiating his unalloyed joy, he turned to Mr. McGuire.

"You wanted to see me, Red?"

"Yeah," answered McGuire worshipfully. "Gee, Big Nose, you got a sock! You just tapped him and he took the count."

"Let's get out of here," growled LeBrett, eying the ring of spectators with a jaundiced eye.

Serrano turned an innocent eye on him. "What's the matter, Charlie? If you think your left—"

Like a man who had the weight of the world on his shoulders, LeBrett heaved a patient sigh. "The left was the nuts," he said dryly. "But cut the clowning. You're always pulling a hippodrome!"

Serrano eyed him from beneath shaggy brows, then punched him affectionately in the ribs. "True to form, eh, Charlie? Always crabbing the act. The trouble with you, Charlie, is that you've got no soul—no—no *esprit*." He pronounced it *es-prit*, looked cagily at LeBrett from one eye to see if the word had gone over.

LeBrett never moved a muscle. "Do we speak to the kid or don't we?" he asked woodenly.

Serrano shook his head sadly, as if there was no more he could do about it, and tucking his arm under the kid's, led the way to the bar.

Young Red insisted that on Mondays—wash day in the McGuire household—he always rushed the growler for Mr. McGuire's better half; and that the can invariably arrived home half empty. Thus assured, Serrano set before him a half dozen hard boiled eggs and a tall glass of beer.

Somewhat fortified by the beverage, the kid began his tale.

"The old lady wants to know if you can spare twenty, Big Nose. It's for the rent. It's a week overdue now and unless—"

"Sure, don't I know?" interrupted Serrano. He slipped a bill of large denomination into the kid's grimy palm. "That's the hell of landlords. How's the old man?"

"Bad," answered McGuire laconically, with an odd tightening of the jaw.

"Hitting the bottle again?" asked LeBrett.

Young McGuire shook his head. "Wrong, Charlie. Hit *with* a bottle."

"A brawl?" questioned Big Nose.

"Murder," said the kid. "A dozen gorillas jumped him. They beat him up bad. The old man gave 'em hell while it lasted, but they put him in the hospital."

Serrano's hard blue eyes narrowed, his hairy nose dilated. He and Terry McGuire had cracked more than one bottle together—more than one thick skull for the greater glory of the Bloody Fourth. And now McGuire, Sr., was in the hospital because a squad of gorillas had gone to work on him. He had to do something about that.

"What's the story, kid?" he asked.

"Trouble down at the yards," answered Red. "Pop says the company's importin' a lot of gorillas to beat the election."

"Election?" puzzled Serrano. "What election?"

Red McGuire looked disdainful. "Sure—you know. This N. R. A. business."

Big Nose was still bewildered and LeBrett elaborated with characteristic brevity. "Section 7 A. The Midwest Packing is forming its own union with a mob of imported gunmen."

Serrano nodded his ponderous head sagely up and down, ran a gnarled fist over the stubble on his chin and chastised the cuspidor with a yard or so of tobacco juice.

"Imported gorillas," he mused in a hushed voice. "Gunmen!" The ancient light of battle flamed to his eyes. "You know, Charlie," he continued, his voice edged with eagerness, "it's been a long time since I swung a beer bottle or a gun."

LeBrett poured two stiff four fingered jolts from the bottle that decorated the table.

"Yeah," he drawled. "It is a neat set-up. Either you join the company union—or else. A lot of good lads in the Fourth took the 'or else.' Mac's in the hospital."

Serrano poured his drink down his cast iron gullet, then shook his head. "You don't have to sell me on the idea, Charlie," he said. "Who's back of it?"

"Skovac. And back of Skovac is Lasker—"

"And back of Lasker is Raymour," finished Serrano. "Is that it?"

LeBrett nodded. "All three bad eggs. You interested?"

Big Nose beamed fondly on his ally. "Charlie," he said, "I've been praying for something like this. I'm getting rusty"— he punched himself in the stomach—"flabby"—he flexed his brawny arms—"I'm getting soft." He patted his hip for the reassuring bulge of his automatic. "From now on we're in this up to our ears. What do you know?"

LeBrett shrugged his shoulders, dragged deep on his cigarette, then waved the butt vaguely through the air. "They tell me Skovac's called a little meeting for his boys down at Webb Hall for tonight. Going to deliver a lecture on the best way to use the boot and a pair of brass knucks."

Serrano rubbed the side of his nose with a broad forefinger and a faraway light gleamed in his eye. LeBrett saw it, groaned.

"Don't say it, Big Nose," he begged. "I been looking forward to a nice, quiet evening."

His plea fell on deaf ears. "Who said it won't be a nice quiet evening?" Serrano demanded. "We're just going down to Webb Hall and listen to Skovac's speech. We won't say a word—not a word." He laid a bill beside the check, scraped back his chair. "Come on, let's go."

Red McGuire crammed the last egg into his bulging cheeks, mumbled around it. "I'm with you, Big Nose."

"The hell you say," retorted Big Nose. "You're going to beat it right home to your old lady."

They paraded through the lobby, emerged through the revolving door on to the sidewalk. Serrano repeated his command.

"Fade, kid. And don't forget to tell your old man that he needn't worry. Big Nose is on the job. Scram!"

McGuire mumbled something that sounded like "Hully Chee"; then with an expression of extreme disgust, thrust his hands into his ragged pockets and shuffled off down the street.

Serrano watched his retreating form for a minute with an admiring eye. "The kid's got the makings," he told LeBrett. "A chip off the old block."

CHAPTER II

Lead Promise

THE foremost cab of the rank at the curb pulled up. Its door swung open as Serrano and LeBrett crossed the sidewalk.

"Where to, Mister?"

"Webb Hall," answered Big Nose as he climbed inside. Still emitting an occasional groan, LeBrett followed, plumped down on the cushions beside him.

The cab swung out from the curb, pulled out into the stream of traffic. LeBrett started to groan again, then broke off abruptly. "I just thought of something," he announced with sudden satisfaction. "We can't get into that meeting, Big Nose. Skovac handed out passes, and we ain't got any. Let's tell the cabby to head for the Bijou instead—there's a new burley show opening there tonight."

Serrano scowled. He glowered in silence as the cab sped down a block, swung around a corner, turned right again. Then suddenly he leaned forward and shoved back the glass panel that separated them from the driver.

"Don't pull right up to the Hall, buddy," he ordered. "Stop half a block this side of the joint."

It was LeBrett's turn to scowl.

"What the—?"

"Never mind. You'll see," Serrano assured him grimly.

Nothing more was said until the taxi pulled up. Serrano rustled his pal out, followed him to the sidewalk. Then his hand went into his pocket, came up with a bill. He waved it under the driver's nose.

"Want to earn this one?" he asked.

The cabby's eyes took in the denomination of the bill, went wide. His head nodded so vigorously it threatened to fly off his shoulders.

"You'll get it," promised Big Nose. "Just stay here for a minute. Leave your engine running."

He took LeBrett's elbow, steered him across the sidewalk and parked him well in the shadows of a darkened doorway. Then he peered out from their vantage point, looked up and down the street.

From all directions, men were converging on the lighted marquee over the entrance of Webb Hall. Singly, in two's and three's, Skovac's gorilla squad was headed for the meeting. A pair of typical specimens ambled down the street toward the watching Serrano. He stepped swiftly back.

"You know what to do, Charlie. Get set!"

He spat on his huge palms, rubbed his hands together.

Footsteps rang hollowly on the pavement, drew nearer. The two unsuspecting gorillas marched abreast of the shadowy doorway.

Long arms reached out from the gloom, iron hands clamped down. The pair were whisked from the sidewalk and jerked unceremoniously into the blackness beyond.

For a hectic moment the silence in the shadowy doorway was broken by hoarse oaths, by the thud of fists, by the sounds of a brief but violent struggle. Then the two gorillas, each with an iron fist at the back of his collar and its mate clutching the seat of his pants, were propelled swiftly across the sidewalk and popped into the waiting cab.

Serrano flung the promised bill at the driver. "There you are, buddy. Get going!"

He slammed the door shut as the taxi jolted away from the curb. As it picked up speed a hand clawed at the rear window and a pale and twisted face glared back at them. Serrano flung a derisive razzberry after it, then he turned to LeBrett and triumphantly waved a crumpled slip of yellow paper.

"I got mine, Charlie. You get yours?"

The whole incident had been accomplished so swiftly, so quietly, that it had drawn no attention. LeBrett produced his loot, regretfully held up two ragged bits of paper. "Mine got torn in the scuffle." Carefully he licked the ragged edges, lovingly pasted the pass together again. "There, that'll hold long enough to hand it over at the door. Did you notice, Big Nose, that these damn things are yellow? I never realized before that Skovac had a sense of humor."

Arm in arm, clutching their precious tickets, they headed for Webb Hall. As they mingled with the others, drew near the entrance, LeBrett turned suspiciously on his companion.

"Remember, you said we were just going to listen."

Serrano looked injured. "I said so, didn't I? You know me, Charlie."

"Yeah," retorted LeBrett. "That's just the trouble."

They turned up their coat collars, pulled the brims of their hats well down over their eyes. They got past the busy ticket taker at the door without any trouble, filed into the big auditorium. The long rows of wooden seats were pretty well filled, but Big Nose jostled and elbowed his way down the aisle, wedged into a space big enough for a midget and shoved until there was room for LeBrett beside him. Blithely he ignored the comments of his outraged neighbors. He was in high good humor, at least for the moment.

He screwed around on his seat, looked back toward the door, then dug his elbow into LeBrett's ribs.

"We got here just in time, Charlie. Look, here comes Skovac himself."

LeBrett looked. They knew Skovac—knew him well. They had tangled with him, and with the mob of scab strike-breakers that he ruled, in the past. And Skovac's memory of those days was not one that he cared to recall. LeBrett summed him up now in one word. "Ape!"

It was a brief description, but an expressive one. Skovac shambled down the aisle with his satellites at his heels. His abnormally long arms dangled loosely from his shoulders. Beetling brows jutted out over close-set eyes and his small ears stuck out from a bullet-shaped head.

As he mounted the raised wooden dais at the end of the hall his motley crew of gunmen, strong-arm crew and other riff-raff raised a hoarse cheer. Serrano fought a sudden impulse, lost—thrust his tongue out and made a loud and inelegant noise.

The heads in their vicinity swung immediately about to glare. Up on the platform Skovac peered, scowling, in their general direction. LeBrett brought a heavy hand down on the back of Serrano's neck, ducked him out of sight, held him there.

Skovac searched the audience for a long moment with a cold stare. Then at last he took his place behind the speaker's stand, cleared his throat. LeBrett eased his hold and Serrano straightened up, his face flushed.

"What the hell's the big idea?" he demanded.

"You damn fool," answered LeBrett, "there's only two of us. Peace and quiet—nerts! I don't feel like being slaughtered. I think I'll go take in that burley show, after all."

Serrano pulled him back as he started to rise. "Hold on, this show'll be better. Remember Terry McGuire."

LeBrett subsided, as Skovac began his little speech.

"Gentlemen." Serrano grimaced. "Gentlemen," Skovac's hoarse voice filled the auditorium, "I didn't get you here tonight to make any fancy speeches. And I'm not going to tell you what the traveling salesman said to the farmer's daughter, or anything like that. We're here on business.

"You boys were hired for a job and I'm going to tell you how we're going to handle that job. But before I get down to practical details, I'm going to give you the straight dope on the whole set-up. You know the employees of the Midwest Packing have been squawking. They're damn lucky they got jobs, but they're growling just the same."

LeBrett, watching Serrano's face closely, suddenly tramped hard on his companion's toe. At the warning, Big Nose's jaw set at a grim angle.

Skovac went on, his language, as he warmed up to his subject, becoming more natural. "These muggs want a union, see? Well, they're going to get a union. Only they got to be kept in line. That's where you guys come in.

"You're going to be members. You're going to have membership cards and all that stuff and you'll rate just as much say-so as these other mugs. I'm warning you right now, the union meetings ain't going to be no picnic. But you're going to take your orders from me. I'm backing you up. I ain't naming no names, but the higher-ups are backing you. The sky's the limit. If the opposition gets tough, a couple of cracked skulls will talk louder than words."

"Not when I say them!"

Serrano's booming voice rang out through the vast hall. For a moment a tense, ominous silence filled the auditorium.

It was broken by a low groan from Charlie LeBrett. "I knew it!" he wailed.

"Who said that?" shouted Skovac.

Serrano shook off LeBrett's restraining hand, climbed deliberately to his feet. Every eye in the place swung to focus on his face.

"I did, punk. Me—Big Nose Serrano. What are you going to do about it?"

Skovac's face darkened. At the ends of his long arms his hands clenched into fists. "You got something to say?"

"Plenty," Big Nose assured him. "And I'll tell you right now. You're a dirty, lousy scab, Skovac. You'd sell your grandmother down the river for a measly quarter. You're out to break the skulls of overworked, underpaid men just because some blood-sucking millionaire's out to squeeze them harder; just because somebody pays you blood money to do it." He flung his arms wide in a reckless, impassioned gesture. "And these yeggs you've collected, these scum—what I said about you goes for them. Double!"

The hushed silence that had fallen over the assemblage, stunned at his audacity, was broken by a low growl. It grew, swelled to a menacing roar. Someone leaped to his feet and the action jerked them all out of their seats. As one man the outraged gorillas converged on this brazen intruder in their midst. On the platform, Skovac shouted in a rage: "Get him!"

In an instant, the interior of Webb Hall was pandemonium itself. With an ominous roar the mob of strikebreakers surged forward.

LeBrett fell automatically into place, back to back against Serrano's broad shoulders. Guns sprouted in their fists. The charge was checked.

Big Nose poised himself lightly on the balls of his feet, swept his heavy automatic around in a slow arc. From smouldering eyes he surveyed the rabble hemming him in. Then his lips curled in magnificent scorn. He raised his booming voice.

"Listen—you muggs! This is a gun—and I know how to use it! It's aching to empty its guts into some of yours. Now if any of you think I'm bluffing. . . ."

He left his threat unfinished—but Death hovered ominously in the room. The tension in the hall built up, charge upon charge, until an explosion was imminent.

"We got to get out of here," grated LeBrett into Serrano's ear. "All hell is going to pop!"

"We'll get out," answered Big Nose, "but first. . . .Stick by me, son." He started to edge out into the aisle.

"Where you going?" moaned LeBrett, lock-stepping after him.

"I got a few words to say to Skovac," answered Serrano heavily. Then he grinned. "And a ditty to sing."

Charlie opened his mouth to protest, then snapped it shut again. He knew from bitter past experience that when Serrano had one of his new musical creations to sing, all hell or high water wouldn't stop him.

LeBrett's finger tightened around the trigger of his gun. What a combination! Lead and lyrics!

But Serrano saw nothing funny in the situation. Boldly—the menacing nozzle of his gun clearing a way for him—he marched up to the platform. With sullen, deep-throated rumblings, the push fell away before his advance. Then with surprising agility for one of his bulk, he vaulted up to the dais. In three long strides he crossed over to Skovac.

Their eyes clashed almost audibly. The crowd in the packed auditorium waited with bated breath for the explosion. And Big Nose did not keep them waiting long. His long left arm shot out, caught Skovac by the slack of his vest and yanked him forward.

"Listen—punk!" snarled Serrano. "This is your first warning—and your last! I'm a man of peace, but unless you call off your dogs—it'll be lilies for Skovac! Get it?"

Skovac's thick lips curled back from yellowed teeth. "I get nothing! If you're looking for hell, I can make plenty of my own. Why, you—"

"Oke!" snarled Big Nose. "I'm starting now!"

Abruptly he released his hold on Skovac's vest. His left arm shot back—then forward with the crushing impact of a battering ram. Skovac took the iron-shod fist on the chin, threw his hands wide, staggered back, then collapsed in a grotesque heap at the far side of the platform.

Serrano stared at him a moment, hopeful that he would rise. But Skovac was out—cold. Then, with a shrug, Big Nose turned to his audience. He executed a mock bow—cleared his throat with a portentous rumble, and expanding his leather-like lungs, broke into full-throated song.

"Lasker's a bum and his men are just
scum.
They'd plug a poor guy for a quarter.
But Big Nose came to call when they
met in Webb Hall
And told 'em to lay off or there'd be
slaughter."

The last notes of the unmelodious ditty were drowned out by a new sound. From outside in the street, came the high pitched wail of a police siren. Then another—and another.

With magnificent disdain, Serrano ignored them. "How was that, Charlie?" he called to LeBrett.

"The berries," growled Charlie. "You'll be singing it from a cell if we don't get out of here."

"We're going—but you wouldn't hurry a gentleman, would you?" grinned Serrano.

Then, with their leveled guns covering their retreat, they backed warily across the stage and slipped out a rear exit.

IN the comparative peace and quiet of McGinnis' back room, they discussed their initial move in their latest campaign. Serrano set down his empty glass of Scotch, beamed fondly up at McGinnis.

"You should have been there, Mac," he chortled. "That song of mine wowed 'em!"

"Sure," grunted LeBrett sarcastically. "It brought the police. Well, now that you've expressed your poetic temperament, I guess I can turn in."

"Like hell you can!" boomed Serrano. "You got a date. We're going places tonight."

McGinnis' eye twinkled. He patted his apron-covered paunch. "If you're on the warpath again, Big Nose, let me in on it. I'm getting fat—sitting on my can around here. And I'm aching for action. What's up?"

Over another bottle, Serrano outlined his campaign. McGinnis listened eagerly, waited in silence until he had finished. Then at last he nodded, started to untie his apron. "Looks like a brawl," he commented dryly. "Count me in. And say—Goldstein was around last night. Wanted to know what you were doing. The Hebe's a handy guy in a brawl and you could use him. Shall I give him a buzz? And where do we go tonight?"

Big Nose grinned fondly at him. "You stick here for now, Mac. Me and Charlie are just going to pay some social calls. But get in touch with Goldstein and the Greek. I may need you boys before I put the skids to Skovac. He's a tough baby." He poured himself a last drink, gurgled it noisily down his throat. "Come on, Charlie, let's get the bus and scram."

LeBrett made a face, dabbed at his blinking eye. "I got a date—with a bed," he said sourly. "That's official."

Serrano shook his head sorrowfully at McGinnis. "A little action and he's got to go to bed!" he snorted. "How about some Peppo tablets, Sunshine? Or a truss? Jeez, it must be hell to get old!"

LeBrett kicked back his chair, stalked to the door. He yanked it open, glared at his pal for a long, disdainful moment. "Well, what the hell are you waiting for?" he demanded angrily. "Is your fanny glued to the chair?"

Serrano grunted, winked broadly at McGinnis and lumbered meekly after him.

CHAPTER III

The Kid Makes a Bull's Eye

MIKE LASKER, racketeering labor boss and master strikebreaker, occupied a suite of dingy offices in the dingier Court Building up on North Clark Street. The locality was a little bit out of Serrano's territory, but now that he had tasted again the salty blood of battle, that wasn't going to stop him.

Once launched on one of his holy crusades, nothing short of a blast from a machine gun could do that.

And thus it was that a half hour after leaving McGinnis', he tooled his sedan expertly to the curb before the shabby entrance to the Court Building. He eased his automatic from his shoulder holster, examined it swiftly with an expert eye, then dropped it casually into the side pocket of his coat.

"This is just a social call, Charlie," he said to LeBrett, seated beside him. "But don't let it get out of hand."

"Hell, no!" grunted LeBrett. "This is one time where we're going to mix business and pleasure—and like it. Let's go."

Always a sartorial gent, Serrano cocked his iron hat at a more jaunty angle, then with an unlit cigar jutting aggressively from his mouth, slid from behind the wheel. Shoulder to shoulder with LeBrett, they pounded across the sidewalk, breezed through the door of the building.

And as it slammed shut behind them with an ominous bang, the dirty, freckled face and wide eyes of Red McGuire stared after them from the rear of Serrano's sedan.

At the head of a long flight of wooden stairs, Big Nose and LeBrett pulled up short before a glass paneled door. Light shone from behind it and through the closed portal came the hum and drone of heavy voices.

"Looks like Lasker is in session," grunted LeBrett, fingering the gun in his pocket.

"Yeah—but did you read this?" answered Serrano disdainfully. With a stubby forefinger he indicated the legend painted on the glass panel of the door.

Michael Lasker
Labor Protective Agency

He snorted; his bulbous nose twitched and his gorilla chest threatened to burst the buttons on his vest. "Looks like we got to do a little protecting on our own."

Savagely he wrenched the knob of the door with his left hand, kicked open the portal with a heavy foot. Backed by LeBrett, he marched across the threshold.

His eyes flared wide, then as suddenly narrowed. The grin on his face broadened to a happy smile. And by his side, the saturnine LeBrett began to whistle unmusically through his teeth the opening bars of *"Just Before the Battle, Mother."*

For their arrival had evidently been expected. They were greeted, not only by Lasker and a dozen of his gorillas but by the menacing guns bulging in their fists.

Serrano rolled his cigar from one corner of his mouth to the other, punched back his derby and rocked back on his heels. He nodded briefly at Lasker. "'Lo, punk," he said. Then slowly he swung his shaggy head around on his bull neck and surveyed the row of menacing faces confronting him. "Nice lot, eh, Charlie," he commented. "Just out of Sunday school." Then his voice hardened. "Why, if it ain't our old friend Peanuts Corbin!"

He took a long stride across the room, pulled up short before a rat-faced individual in a slouch hat. With a magnificent contempt he ignored the heavy automatic in Corbin's fist.

"Still slinging a gun for pay, eh, rat?" he snarled. Abruptly he took the knot of Corbin's tie, yanked it tight and hard up against the gunman's Adam's apple.

Corbin went blue in the face—then white. His upper lip quivered and little beads of sweat popped out on his forehead.

"You'll never die that way, scum!" grated Serrano. "You'll get yours with a slug of lead."

"Try that again and by God—"

"Nuts! You haven't got the guts."

Big Nose turned to the next man, crooked his forefinger and plucked him under the nose. "Cocky Smith—and Blackie Schwartz—and Ike Vogel!" He turned, swaggered back across the room to Lasker, hitched his bulk onto a corner of Lasker's desk. "You're dumber than I thought, mug, if you think you can run this racket with that outfit."

Lasker's tawny eyes were twin opals of hate. With an effort he controlled the twitching of his lips. "It's a nice routine, Serrano," he said heavily. "Go ahead. Make a monkey of yourself. It's your last play!"

Serrano laughed. "Last?" He scraped a match across the top of Lasker's desk, applied it to the tip of his cigar. With a sigh he erupted a heavy cloud of blue smoke. "Hell, Lasker, I'm just beginning. Me and Charlie came up here to give you a break. Your racket is through, see? You're washed up. If you want to take it that way—swell! If you don't. . ." He turned to LeBrett. "What do you say, Charlie?"

"I'm hoping he don't," grated LeBrett.

Lasker's thin lips pulled back in a sneer. "And you're getting your wish. You two mugs have made one wrong play too many." His gun edged up an inch and his finger tightened perceptibly on the trigger. "Take 'em, boys."

Serrano and LeBrett were taken. That is, their guns were expertly frisked from their pockets.

Big Nose flicked ashes across Lasker's immaculate vest. "That takes a load off my mind," he sighed wearily. "I hate to take advantage of rats. That makes the odds about even." Coolly he counted noses. "Yeah, that's about right. Me and Charlie against you and the mob. Well, when does the funny stuff begin?"

Lasker licked his thin lips wolfishly. "Just as soon as Skovac gets here. He wants to work out on you a little before you get it." Slowly he stood up, kicked back his chair. Then, with a sudden movement, he sank the nozzle of his gun deep into Serrano's navel. "Your number is up, big boy," he said in a hard voice. "You've tangled with me for the last time."

Their eyes met and held, clashed audibly. Serrano's nostrils dilated wide and Lasker's finger was white and tense on the trigger.

Death trembled in the room!

Death from the gaping nozzle of Lasker's automatic—and Death from yet another source! Big Nose and LeBrett were lined up, their backs to the door. Confronting them, facing the portal, was Lasker and his men. In the rear wall, behind the mobsters, was a window.

And there, peering through the dirty glass, was the even more dirty face of Red McGuire. And more important still, clutched in his grimy right hand was a long barreled, blue-steel Smith and Wesson.

There was something familiar about that gun. Big Nose could have laughed out loud. With a mighty effort he controlled the impulse, caught the kid's eye, then turned casually to LeBrett. One glance was enough to tell him that his ally had also seen the rescuing angel at the window.

"It's a pretty set-up," grinned Serrano. "What do you say?"

"I'm not asking for any more," answered LeBrett. "This ought to be good."

"It'll be better when Skovac gets here," snarled Lasker.

Big Nose beamed on him fondly. "Want to lay odds?"

"Sure!" snarled Lasker. "Only it's going to be hell to collect from a stiff!"

"Don't I know!" mocked Serrano. Casually he raised his arm, inserted his little finger in his ear—pointed his thumb at the light overhead—and gave the kid the nod.

Young McGuire got his cue, and three things happened simultaneously — or almost simultaneously. Holding the heavy automatic in his two hands, he elevated the muzzle, drew a swift bead on the large light fixture and squeezed the trigger.

Flame and lead erupted from the nozzle—and with a crescendo tinkle of breaking glass, the room was plunged into darkness. Young Red had scored a bull's eye.

Fearing a rear attack, Lasker's men whirled at the crack of the automatic. Their guns belched and a withering cross-fire converged on the fire-escape where the kid had been but a moment before.

Big Nose was swift to take advantage of the momentary confusion. His fist was still at his ear. Now, with the crushing force of a pile driver, it shot forward. It was as expertly aimed as McGuire's bullet and Mr. Lasker's jaw crumpled beneath the blow.

LeBrett deftly caught the automatic as it dribbled from the racketeer's nerveless fingers. Then, flat on their stomachs, he and Serrano began a hurried retreat to the door.

The attack of the gunmen shifted from the window to the portal. Lead criss-crossed the room. The swaying smoke of gun-fire hung over the scene like a shroud.

But LeBrett held his fire until he and Big Nose were across the portal. Then he squeezed lead very rapidly in a vicious blast to check a premature rush on the door.

They hit the stairs running, skidded down the long flight, and as the outer door slammed shut behind them, Serrano's booming bass floated back in derisive challenge.

"Lasker's scabs are after the packers
Because the bosses slip 'em a few
lousy smackers.
With brass knucks and cannons they
think that they're swell,
But Big Nose Serrano will send 'em
to hell!"

"How's that, Charlie?" he bellowed. "Right out of my head!"

"I'll say you're out of your head," grunted LeBrett the unappreciative. "The car—fast!"

Young McGuire himself swung open the door of their sedan as they swept across the sidewalk and with the crescendo scream of police sirens drowning out the crash of guns that still echoed from Lasker's office, they got away from there.

CHAPTER IV

Serrano Lays Down the Law

MR. McGUIRE'S story was simplicity itself. As Serrano raced the sedan north on Michigan Boulevard, he elaborated on the details. After delivering the bill to his old lady, he had picked up Serrano's trail at McGinnis'. And knowing Big Nose of old, he knew that hell was about to pop. He had decided to be in on the popping.

He had followed Serrano and LeBrett to the garage and while they were inspecting the tires, had slipped into the back of the car. Later, when they had gone up to Lasker's office—and nothing had happened—and they hadn't come down, he had decided that something was wrong.

He had investigated, via the rear fire-escape, armed with the Smith and Wesson he had found in the car.

"I ought to lam you for disobeying orders," growled Big Nose. Then, as McGuire's eyes went wide in hurt surprise, he brought his ham-like hand down on the kid's shoulders in a whack that sent the breath whistling from his body. "But I'm going to buy you a beer instead!

McGuire recovered from a fit of coughing, came up beaming. "Then I'm one of the boys now, eh, Big Nose?"

"You sure are." Serrano turned solemnly toward LeBrett. "There's a new partner in the firm now, Charlie. Shake on it."

Ceremoniously, LeBrett enclosed a grimy paw in his own calloused one, pumped the kid's thin arm up and down. McGuire's skinny chest puffed out, strained at the one button that held his ragged coat together.

"I'll take that beer down at McGinnis' joint, Big Nose," he said easily. "Let's go."

"Not tonight—it's too late. I'm taking you right home to your Ma. But get all dolled up bright and early, kid. There's another social call on the list—a real society visit this time—and now that you're a partner you better come along. I'll be around to pick you up." Serrano, amused with the new set-up, chuckled. Then he sobered. "But this time, Red," he added warningly, "no sling-shots, no water pistols, no stink bombs—and no sub-machine guns."

WHEN Serrano's big sedan pulled up before the McGuire tenement at ten the following morning, Red was already ensconced upon the littered stoop. He had, in fact, been waiting impatiently there for the past three hours, not daring to leave his post.

He hurdled down three steps, then remembering his lately-acquired dignity, slowed down to a bold swagger as he crossed the sidewalk. He greeted his partners with the proper formality and accepted a seat beside his idol at the wheel. Big Nose surveyed him critically. The dolling-up that he managed consisted mainly of a vain attempt to plaster down an unruly red thatch with copious applications of water. The result was not exactly successful, but Serrano nodded his approval.

"You look swell, kid. Raymour'll be tickled to make your acquaintance."

The car got under way, headed toward the fashionable precincts of the

Lake Shore Drive. McGuire's newly-acquired nonchalance left him. His mouth gaped.

"You mean—you mean Old Man Raymour—the Big Boss of the Mid-west?"

"Sure. I told you we were crashing into society today."

Red's favorite expression came muffled, strangled. "Hully Chee!"

This was something he hadn't bargained for. Being the partner of Serrano and LeBrett was going to be a far different matter from what he had fondly expected. He subsided back against the cushions to ponder this new angle.

The journey was made in silence. Big Nose, well pleased with the hectic start of his latest crusade, was occupied with no more serious a problem than finding a word to rhyme with "Union." He wondered whether "onion" wouldn't do, in a pinch. LeBrett, from his solitary grandeur on the back seat, was critically comparing the feminine ankles and calves revealed by a brisk breeze from the Lake. Young McGuire was constructing a mental picture of Old Man Raymour from what that gentleman's employees had said about him. He conjured up a saturnine, grinning face with green eyes and sharp horns projecting from the forehead. He was a little doubtful, though, whether the guy really did have a long tail.

They swung at last into a graveled driveway, pulled up before an imposing gray stone mansion. Serrano led the way up the steps to the front door, squashed a broad thumb on the buzzer beside the portal.

A few moments later the door swung inward and a liveried butler peered out at them. When his eyes fell upon Red McGuire, they blinked three times in rapid succession.

"Mister Raymour in?" demanded Big Nose.

"Er—I'll see," answered the butler, uncertainly. "You have an appointment, perhaps?"

Big Nose squared his broad shoulders belligerently. "Appointment, hell," he snorted. "Big Nose Serrano and the—uh—committee are calling. He'll see us."

The flunkey took another look. "Just a minute, Mr. Serrano. I'll see if he's in."

He started to close the door.

That was a mistake. It didn't quite close, blocked by Big Nose's size twelve boot. Serrano shoved the portal roughly inward. His huge hand shot out, grasped a handful of mauve cloth and brass buttons that was the butler's coat front. He heaved, raised the gasping flunkey to his tiptoes, thrust his glowering face into the other's terrified one.

"Nobody closes doors in my nose, you," he growled. "It's a swell nose, a handsome nose, a nice nose. Maybe you don't like it?" he inquired hopefully.

Knowles, the Raymour butler, did not know what was common knowledge in the Bloody Fourth Ward. He did not know that Serrano was extremely sensitive about the prodigious organ that had given him his nickname; did not know that although Serrano joked about it freely himself, it was sudden death for the stranger who dared a wisecrack. Fortunately for Knowles, he was spared the test of his diplomacy.

"It's a lovely nose, really," a low, musical voice broke the tense silence.

Serrano dropped the flunkey back to his heels, whirled abruptly about. A slim, patrician girl was descending the stairs that led from the floor above. She was clad in a simple dress of blue and her honey-colored hair was drawn back into a loose knot at the nape of her neck. Big Nose watched her admiringly as she approached.

"Well?" she inquired coolly. "Surely you didn't come here to get Knowles' opinion of your good looks?"

Despite her calm demeanor, Serrano sensed the twinkle behind her gray eyes. Unabashed, he executed a flourishing bow. "No, mam. I don't give a—I don't care what the gent thinks. We came to see Old Man Raymour."

She made a slight gesture to Knowles, who gratefully vanished from the scene. Red McGuire could not resist the impulse to thumb his nose after the butler's retreating back.

"Old—ah—Mr. Raymour is my father. I'm Joan Raymour."

Serrano bowed again. "Pleased to meet you, Joan. Let me make you acquainted with Charlie LeBrett and Mr. Red McGuire."

The girl acknowledged the introductions, then turned to a door at the end of the hall. "My father's in the library," she said over her shoulder as she led the way. "He'll be delighted to see you."

"And how," grunted LeBrett under his breath.

They filed inside after her, entered a large, luxuriously-furnished room. A stout, pompous, gray-haired man sat behind the broad mahogany table that served him as a desk. He looked up as they entered, stared at the incongruous trio.

"Mr. Serrano, Mr. LeBrett and Mr. McGuire," Joan Raymour told him. She turned to Big Nose. "Speak up."

As she stepped aside, Big Nose stalked up to the table. He looked curiously at the man who was the big boss, the head of the Midwest Packing Company. He looked at the pouches under Raymour's eyes, at the thin, close-set lips, at the sleek paunch that bulged out to touch the table edge. The girl was promptly forgotten.

"I'm Big Nose Serrano—from the Fourth Ward," he boomed. "Maybe you've heard of me, Mister?"

Raymour glared. "I have. Lasker called me up this morning. I've heard all about your crazy antics." He scraped back his chair, climbed to his feet. "But you're going too far when you come barging into my home. Get out!" He pointed an imperious finger toward the door.

Serrano's bulbous nose twitched, turned a shade deeper crimson. It was a warning signal, had Raymour known it. With an effort Big Nose controlled himself.

"Not yet—I'll go when I'm damn good and ready," he retorted. "Listen, Raymour, I'm giving you a break. I came up here to talk to you, to appeal to you. You're piling up a mess of trouble. Give your workingmen a break and you'll do yourself a favor at the same time. Give them decent wages, give them shorter hours, give them better working conditions. Give them their union—on the level, not peppered with Skovac's gorillas."

Raymour's flabby face grew mottled. His hands clenched on the table top. "How dare you come here and talk like that to me?" he demanded. "I'll call the police and have you thrown out like the hoodlum you are. I'm running my own business and no bully Ward boss is going to poke his nose into it."

The word "nose" was fatal. Serrano quivered in every mighty muscle. He leaned across the table, prodded a rigid forefinger deep into Raymour's navel.

"I gave you a break, but you wouldn't take it. You think that because you got millions you can get away with murder. You use your dirty dollars to hire thugs like Lasker and Skovac to do your dirty work for you." His voice rose to a thunderous bellow. "You're not going to get away with it, Raymour. I'll smash Lasker, just like this." His huge fist smote the table a mighty blow that set papers and inkwell dancing. "I'll wipe out Skovac and every last one of his cut-throat crew. And then—God help you!"

He swung abruptly on his heel, marched toward the door. Raymour, two degrees removed from apoplexy, glared after him in impotent speechless rage.

With LeBrett and the irrepressible Red swaggering in his wake, Serrano strode through the hall. As he reached for the knob of the front door, he pulled up to an abrupt halt as a voice floated after him.

"Mr. Serrano, you forgot to say good-bye. Is that nice?"

He turned, thrust his companions aside and walked back to meet the girl who had followed them. The angry flush died from his face.

"I'm sorry, sister," he mumbled sheepishly. "I forgot he was your old man."

"I've never seen anyone talk back to him before," she told him. "It was a rare treat, really."

Serrano brightened again. "I hadn't ought to have said what I did," he explained. "But I got hot under the collar."

"Father's all right," she assured him. "I don't know what this is all about. But if you knew him as well as I do, you'd know he's got a big heart under his domineering manner."

Serrano brazenly chucked her under the chin. "You know, sister, you and I are going to get along. I'll give you a buzz sometime. So long, baby."

He waved an airy farewell, ushered his partners outside and followed them. A blithe whistle piped from his lips as he clattered down the steps, wedged behind the wheel of the sedan, sprayed gravel from the wheels as he headed out of the driveway.

Young McGuire voiced his thoughts aloud. "Ain't she a lulu?"

The whistle died on Big Nose's lips. He looked suspiciously at the kid's face, saw the freckled countenance set in a dreamy, reminiscent grin. "What the hell you grinning at?" he demanded.

"She winked at me," breathed Red ecstatically. "A real big wink, just as I was going out the door."

Big Nose steered dextrously with his left hand, waved an admonishing forefinger under the kid's snub nose. "Nix, kid, lay off. The partner business don't hold good where the dames are concerned. She's mine, see?"

CHAPTER V

The Snatch

"THE poor working man," snorted LeBrett.

"I always did like blondes especially," sighed Serrano.

"Old Man Raymour's her father," reminded LeBrett.

"I don't care if she's the daughter of the devil himself," answered Big Nose. "If they have a little of the Old Nick in them, the better."

"She's kidding the pants off you," said LeBrett sourly.

"I tell you this baby's regular—the real goods." Serrano was indignant. He rolled off the bed where he had been lying, indulging in romantic day dreams, and began to pace the floor of their room. He stopped in mid-stride and glared challengingly at his partner in crime. "A century against a shot of rye says I can date her up—tonight."

LeBrett hooked a long leg over the arm of his chair, squinted thoughtfully at the half-filled glass in his hand. "Of all the sucker bets—go ahead, big boy, do your stuff."

Serrano stalked to the telephone, thumbed through the book to the R's, found the number. Inserting a pudgy forefinger, he dialed it, jammed the receiver against a cauliflowered ear and waited impatiently for the call to go through.

A buzzing voice came over the wire at last. He scowled at the wall over LeBrett's head.

"You *would* answer. Listen, you, tell Miss Raymour that Mister Serrano's calling. And don't tell me that she's not in or I'll come up and break your damn neck."

He drummed his fingers impatiently on the base of the instrument. A few moments later the wire buzzed again. The drumming ceased abruptly.

"Hello, baby. This is Big Nose Serrano. Feel like stepping tonight? What do you say we go places?" He paused, held his breath, then beamed broadly at LeBrett. "Swell," he boomed heartily into the telephone. "Listen, I'll wait for you in the lobby downstairs. I'm at the Royale. Make it snappy, eh?"

He hung up, swaggered across the room, took the unfinished drink from LeBrett's hand and tossed it off in one gulp. "Now what have you got to say, you old crepe-hanger? Where's my hat and coat—she's coming right over. You can buy me that drink later."

"It'll keep." LeBrett shrugged. "She ain't here yet."

DOWN in the ornate, palm-decorated lobby, Serrano tossed away the stub of his fourth cigar. For the tenth time in as many minutes he looked at the clock over the clerk's desk and the scowl on his face deepened. He started for the elevators, gave vent to an explosive "Damn" and turned back. LeBrett was waiting upstairs and Big Nose was in no mood, just then, for any "I-told-you-so's." Once more he fell to pacing the lobby.

His bitter meditations were interrupted by a heavy hand that clamped like a vise on his arm. He turned his head and looked into the face of Detective Marty Flynn.

"Sorry, Big Nose," explained the detective. "But you're wanted down at Headquarters."

"What the hell—what's up?" demanded Serrano.

"I'll explain on the way," answered Flynn. "Let's go."

"You'll explain right now. Speak your little piece, Marty."

Flynn waved his hands helplessly. "Be reasonable, Big Nose. I can't help this—orders is orders. Old Morton Raymour's daughter is gone and—"

It was Serrano's turn to grip the other's arm. "Say that again!"

"His daughter is gone and their butler says she went to meet you. The old gent's wild, says to find you both. Where is she, Big Nose?"

Serrano groaned. "I wish to God

I knew. But I'll find her, if I have to bust the town wide open."

"You're coming with me. The other boys'll find her, don't worry."

Serrano didn't budge. The glimmer of an idea awoke in his brain. His jaw set at a grim angle. "I got a hunch, Marty. I think I know where to look."

Flynn shook his head. "No, you don't. I'm taking you to Headquarters. Raymour's got plenty drag and I don't want my job knocked out from under me. I know you, Big Nose, and I hate like hell to—"

Before Serrano sensed his intention, Flynn made a swift move. There was a sharp click and a slim bracelet of cold steel encircled Big Nose's wrist. Flynn nudged him toward the door.

"Don't blow up, Big Nose. I got to do it."

Serrano's brain seethed. Blindly, mechanically, he stumbled from the hotel, allowed Flynn to herd him across the sidewalk and into a waiting cab. They got under way with a jerk that sat him down hard on the cushions. The jolt was all he needed to crystallize the milling thoughts that ran riot through his consciousness.

He could not let himself be led, like a sheep, into Headquarters. He could not be held there, impotent, helpless, while others searched for Joan Raymour. He had to get away from Flynn, immediately.

He rubbed his nose with his free hand, scratched behind his ear, then reached casually for his pocket. "Got a match, Marty?"

His easy manner fooled Flynn, for a moment. But that moment was all Serrano needed. His hand flashed up, the glow from a street lamp shone for a moment on blued steel, then his arm came down in a short, vicious arc. The heavy butt of his gun struck Flynn's temple with a brief thud and the detective collapsed limply on the cushions.

"Sorry, Marty," Big Nose muttered as he fumbled in Flynn's pockets, "But *I* had to do *that*."

The driver had not heard the single dull thud of the blow. The cab sped steadily through the streets. Serrano's probing fingers found the key, inserted it in the lock of the handcuffs and clicked the bracelet open.

The first intimation the cabby had that something had gone amiss, was the icy touch of steel at the back of his neck. His hands froze on the wheel as Serrano's gruff voice sounded in his ear.

"Slow down at the next corner."

He did as he was bid. As his foot eased off the gas pedal, Serrano swung open the rear door, stepped onto the running board and landed, staggering, in the gutter. He brandished the weapon, bellowed after the cab. "Keep going!"

As the winking red tail-lights of the taxi disappeared down the street, Big Nose sprinted for the cigar store at the corner. He wedged himself into a telephone booth, dropped a coin into the slot and dialed the number of the Royale Hotel.

IN a veritable hail of gravel, the big sedan roared up the driveway and pulled up to a sudden halt before the entrance to Raymour's home. Serrano and LeBrett piled out of the machine, barged up the steps and round the door open. Men milled around in the hallway, reporters representing every paper in the city. The door to the library was closed and Knowles, pallid and perspiring, stood guard before it.

The abrupt entrance of Big Nose Serrano produced a sensation. The newshounds leaped at him in a mass.

"Big Nose—what's the dope?"

"What happened?"

"Where is she?"

Serrano brushed them impatiently aside, shouldered his way to where the butler stood petrified at his post. "Get out of the way!"

If the devil himself had suddenly popped up before him, Knowles could not have moved a finger. He stood like a graven image, gaping, helpless. With a low growl Serrano plucked him away from the door grasped the knob.

"Stay here, Charlie. Keep everybody out."

He swung the portal inward, stepped across the threshold and closed it behind him. Seated at his desk was Raymour. His flabby jowls were ashen, his pouchy eyes lack-lustre. They focused unseeingly on the broad form of Serrano for a moment, then, as recognition flooded them, Raymour leaped to his feet with a cry.

"You!" he pointed a trembling finger. "Where's my daughter? Where's Joan?"

"I haven't seen her."

Raymour's eyes rolled wildly. "You're lying. She sneaked off to meet you. Where is she?"

"I told you I haven't seen her."

Raymour collapsed like a pricked balloon. He sank back limply into his chair. Serrano strode across the room, confronted him coldly.

"I got a good hunch who's got her, though."

Raymour bounced up again. "Who —for God's sake?"

"Your own hired killers—Skovac and Lasker."

"You're mad." Raymour ran his hands wildly through his hair. "What would they kidnap Joan for?"

Serrano shrugged. "Lots of reasons. Pin it on me and get me out of the way, for one. Bleed you white, for another. Or—you got drag in this town—they could force you to back up their play until they ran every racket in the city. Take your choice." He looked coldly into Raymour's stricken face. "They wouldn't take her to Lasker's office. Where would they go?"

Raymour's bloodless lips alone moved. "The garage," he mumbled. "Skovac has a place down by the river—an old garage at the corner of McMaster and Lowe. His headquarters." Suddenly he found the use of his limbs. He stumbled toward the telephone on his desk. "The police—"

Serrano jerked the instrument from his trembling hands. "The hell with the cops! This is my job. I'll get her back for you."

Swiftly he dialed a number, the number of McGinnis' cafe. The cheery voice of the Irishman answered him. "Get Goldstein—get all the boys you can round up," ordered Serrano. "Load 'em with artillery and shoot 'em down to McMaster and Lowe. We're going to clean up Skovac and his rats."

He banged the receiver back on the hook. McGinnis would ask no questions. Big Nose grasped Raymour by the elbow. "Come on, Mister. You can have a ringside seat for the finish. It'll do you good. It'll give you an idea what you were monkeying with when you hired Skovac and Lasker."

He steered the hapless man toward the door, out into the hall where they were instantly surrounded by the frantic reporters.

"Trail along if you want to," Serrano told them, as LeBrett cleared a path to the outer door. "You'll get a yarn that'll fill the front page."

CHAPTER VI

The Kiss-off

AS he turned down McMaster Street, Serrano slowed his speed until the roar of the powerful motor died to a low hum. He thrust his arm out of the window, waggled a huge hand. The trailing reporters took the warning, dropped back as the sedan slid on to the rendezvous.

A half block from their destination three cars were pulled up at the curb. McGinnis had responded faithfully to the S.O.S. Big Nose eased the sedan in ahead of the foremost car, piled out onto the sidewalk. He and LeBrett were promptly surrounded by McGregor, Joe Goldstein, and the mob that Serrano had ruled in the hectic, flaming days of Prohibition.

Big Nose was in his element. He knew these men, knew they would follow him through hell and high water. His eyes gleamed as he saw they were bristling with weapons. He beamed fondly around at the ring of familiar faces.

"Just like old times, eh, boys? We're going to have a swell blowout, together, just like in the old days. Only we got a job to do, first." They gathered closer about him, waiting for orders. "There's a dame in that place," he warned them. "We got to think of her first. If they don't put up a fight, I'll massacre the first one of you that starts something. But if they do get tough—give 'em hell."

A low, subdued cheer answered him. He brandished his automatic. "I'll lead the band. The rest of you take your cue from me."

Old Man Raymour was forgotten, left in the parked sedan. Well in the van of his cohorts, Serrano strode down the gloomy street, headed for the ramshackle old garage on the corner. Stray gleams of light showed from beyond its sagging shutters. Lounging against the door, smoking a cigarette, stood one of Skovac's men.

Some sixth sense warned the lookout of Big Nose's approach. The cigarette dropped in a hissing shower of sparks as he whirled around. The glow of light from the corner street lamp illuminated the features of Big Nose Serrano.

The guard waited for no more. Without warning, without challenge, he blazed away. The staccato report of his gun echoed in the silent street and Serrano's hat was whisked neatly from his head.

Big Nose's decision had been made for him. His gun convulsed, belched flame—and the lookout toppled limply from his post. Serrano's war whoop rang out above the crash of gunfire and at the signal, his eager crew came running to the fray.

The ancient door was riddled with a fusillade of bullets, assaulted by burly shoulders. It burst inward under the impact and Serrano and his men barged into the garage.

Skovac's gorillas met them with flaming lead. In an instant the building was a chaos of spitting guns, of shouts and curses, of milling men. Big Nose heard the voice of Skovac himself, yelling orders in a hoarse voice above the din. With swinging fist and spouting gun he battled his way in that direction.

"Lay off him!" he bellowed to his comrades. "He's mine!"

Skovac saw him coming. Serrano saw the swift fear flash in the strikebreaker's eyes, saw his gun muzzle come up and gape hungrily in his direction. Their guns roared as one. A bullet ploughed a burning path across Serrano's temple. Warm blood spurted from the wound, trickled into his eyes, dissolved everything into a blinding red mist. He dabbed at the crimson stream with the back of his hand and as his vision cleared, he saw Skovac lying limp and twisted on the floor of the garage.

From somewhere up above came a single, shrill scream — abruptly choked off. Big Nose's head jerked up as he swept a glance about him. Through the blue cloud of gun smoke that hung like a pall in the air, he saw a rickety flight of stairs leading upward. LeBrett covered his charge for the stairs.

The wooden slats creaked under his weight as he pounded upward. He burst open a door at the head of the stairs and found himself face to face with a wild-eyed, disheveled Lasker. Big Nose's finger constricted on the trigger and a hollow click echoed in his ears. His gun was empty.

Lasker's face contorted in savage hate. Slowly, deliberately, he drew a bead on Serrano's belt buckle.

"You've butted in for the last time, Big Nose," he said hoarsely. "Now—take it!"

A streak of blue and gold flashed across the room. A white hand struck Lasker's elbow. His gun exploded and plaster sprayed down from the ceiling. Then the useless weapon flew from Serrano's fingers, struck square on Lasker's scowling brow. His knees buckled and he slid limply to the floor.

Big Nose shoved his unconscious body out of the way with a callous boot, turned to the girl. Her dress was torn, her hair cascaded in touseled glory over her bare shoulders, but her eyes were shining.

"You're a wow, sister," he said admiringly. Then, as the highest compliment he could offer, he added: "You'd make a swell partner, baby."

And Joan Raymour, heiress to the Midwest Packing millions, asked softly: "Do you really think so, Big Nose?"

The crackle of gunfire downstairs had ceased and heavy footsteps clattered up the stairs. They were instantly surrounded. The horde of reporters belabored Serrano with a barrage of questions. He stayed them with an upraised hand.

"I got an inspiration," he announced. "I'll give you the whole story—in a little ditty I just made up. It goes like this." He threw back his shoulders, winked at the girl and burst into rollicking song.

"A bunch of rats all armed with gats
Shanghai'd a swell-looking lady.
They were mugs that I hate so I
crashed the gate
And rescued a million dollar baby."

The reporters whooped in glee, snatched out notebooks and begged for an encore. Modestly Serrano obliged and while he rocked the room with his booming bass, scratching pencils recorded the immortal lines for posterity.

As the last note died away, there was a stir at the head of the stairs. The men there parted and Old Man Raymour, forgotten in the excitement, stepped into the room. His hands came up, trembling, as he stumbled over to meet his daughter.

Big Nose watched their happy embrace with thoughtful eyes. He rubbed the side of his Gargantuan nose with his forefinger a moment, then he brightened.

"Yeah," he announced. "I almost forgot. You can run a statement from Mr. Raymour. The employees of the Midwest Packing Company are going to have their union. They're going to get a higher wage scale, shorter hours, better working conditions. Their spokesmen will arrange the details with Mr. Raymour tomorrow. Ain't that right, Mr. Raymour?"

For an instant the color rose in Raymour's face like the red fluid in a thermometer. Then slowly it subsided again. He looked at his daughter, then faced the reporters. "Yes, that's right. I'll sign that statement."

LeBrett sighed. "It was fun while it lasted," he said regretfully. "One of you mugs take care of Lasker there. I see he's coming to. And you, Big Nose, I owe you a drink. Let's go, I could use one myself."

"Just a minute," said Serrano. "You don't owe it to me, yet." He crossed over to Joan Raymour. "Baby, I promised this push a blowout. It'll be in Clancy's Hall tomorrow night. A swell affair—soup and fish and everything. Will you come?"

She nodded, smiling.

Big Nose beamed. He took LeBrett's elbow. "That's settled. Let's get that drink. And after we have that one, we'll have another. And another. And another . . ."

INSIDE JOB

By PRESTON GRADY

ALL the lights had been turned out in the lobby except a couple behind the desk and one over one of those little game tables where you pull a plunger and knock a ball up and see what slots it goes into. The blond young clerk was looking at pictures in a magazine. The elevator started to come down slow, kind of wheezing.

I guessed it was from the fourth floor. You could tell, the thing ran so slow. Besides, the hotel wasn't but six stories high, and the only reason it was that high was because the rich Yankees gave the town a play in the winter. Polo and all that stuff.

The elevator stopped at the lobby, the door opened, and this narrow-shouldered bimbo with the long face and the little pug nose that seemed to have got there by mistake came out with the Negro bell-hop who had run the car behind him.

In his shirt sleeves, this pug-nosed guy came up to the desk and asked: "Got any cigarettes?"

I could hear him because I had turned the radio down low.

The clerk said, "Sure," and pulled open the drawer where he kept a few assorted packages. The cigar stand was closed. It was after three o'clock in the morning. "What kind?"

Leaning across the desk so he could see into the drawer, the pug-nosed guy named a brand. The clerk took it out and handed it to him. The pug-nosed guy paid, tore the package open and got out a cigarette.

"Can't sleep," he said out of the cup formed by his hands as he lit the cigarette. "Too damned hot."

"Yeah," the clerk agreed without much interest, and started back to turning the pages of the magazine.

"Besides," the pug-nosed guy went on, "I'm out of liquor. If I had a stiff drink I might be able to get some sleep. But I'm out. Where can I get a pint?"

The clerk shrugged and said: "We still got prohibition in this state, mister." He turned and went behind the partition and started checking over some registration cards or something like that. I couldn't see exactly what he was doing.

Smoke dribbled from the pug-nosed guy's nostrils. He took the cigarette out of his mouth and spoke to the Negro who sat on a bench.

"Can you get me a pint of decent liquor, shine? Not corn?"

The shine didn't say anything. But after a second he got up and strolled around the corner of the elevator bank, toward a water cooler that was in the deep shadows at the back of the lobby. This pug-nosed guy didn't follow him. The shine didn't want to miss a sale, though, so he came up toward the front of the lobby where I was. It was pretty dim up there too.

Finally the pug-nosed guy followed. They were about a dozen feet away from me. The pug-nosed guy asked his question all over again and the answer he got was this:

"Sho', mister, I'll get it for you. But you shouldn't oughta ask me that way in front of the clerk. 'Course he knows I sells it and all that, but just the same he ain't *s'posed* to know nothin' about it. What kind you want?"

"What kind you got?"

The shine named half a dozen popular brands. The pug-nosed guy asked for a pint of one of them and sat down right where he was in one of the heavy leather-covered chairs. This is all very important now and I want you to pay close attention on account of what happened afterward. Anyhow, he could see the shine going down a stairway to the basement.

After a while the shine came back up with a package in his hand, crossed to where the pug-nosed guy sat, and stood there with one of those large pillars concealing him from the desk as he handed the package over.

"Three dollars."

The pug-nosed guy gave him the money and the shine went back and sat down on the bench, utterly expressionless. With his face all screwed up in a frown, the pug-nosed guy tore the package open—it was one of those patented pasteboard containers where you have to tear it open to get to the bottle—and threw the wrapping on the floor and uncapped the bottle. He took a long drink right out of the bottle. He saw me then, but he didn't pay any attention to me.

He stuck the bottle in his hip pocket and started to get up. He threw his cigarette into the stone vase full of sand.

The swing door at the front was pushed inward and Brinkley came in. Brinkley was the Chief of Police in this town. He was a broad-faced tough guy with a lot of curly hair that stood high on his forehead. He came in and stopped and looked around. What he was doing up at that time of night I don't know, but there he was, as big as you please. It gave me a pain just to look at him.

He came across and planted himself right square in front of the pug-nosed guy, fists on hips, and stuck out his chin like an ape.

This was getting interesting, because I already had the pug-nosed guy sized up for a red hot. I'd seen him when he checked in about midnight, and there was something about him you could tell he was red hot. He said:

"What's eating you, flattie?"

Brinkley said: "Just like that, huh? How'd you know I was a copper?"

A thin, dry smile sort of twisted the pug-nosed guy's lips. "You can tell a skunk by the way he smells. You can tell a copper pretty near the same way." And the pug-nosed guy just stood there with that ugly grin on his face.

Brinkley knocked him down and said: "Get out of town, Shane! We don't want you around here. Get out of town as quick as you can."

Shane got up slow. His pug nose was bloody, but he was as cool as a cucumber. "I don't believe we've met socially." He lifted his eyebrows in mock politeness. "Yet—you seem to know my name."

"One of them, yes. You've got a few others—Wilson, Jarrett, Ingram, Bryan. I wouldn't even know which one you're registered under here. But our night patrolman saw you and recognized you from your picture on a police dodger and phoned me about it, and we don't like it, see? So scram!"

"What's the objection, hayseed? I'm perfectly peaceful, you know."

"Peaceful!" Brinkley sneered. "Peaceful like a box of dynamite! You're on the lam from a bunch of your hoodlum buddies because you crossed 'em on the split from a bank job in Ohio. You thought you'd use this burg for a hide-out. You got a record that reaches from Sing Sing to San Quentin. You're a lousy rat. We haven't got anything on you, but by God if you don't get out of town quick we'll jug you if we have to frame you for it . . . What's that in your hip pocket?"

Shane said: "Liquor."

Brinkley looked around the lobby and spotted me and the clerk and the bell-hop.

"Come over here," he called. "All of you!"

I went over and the others did too. Brinkley patted the bottle on Shane's hip. "See that?" He took the bottle out. It was a wonder it hadn't busted when Shane hit the floor. "That's evidence," Brinkley said. "I just wanted you to see it—see me take it off him. He's a lousy double-crossing rat and we don't want him around here. If he isn't out of town within an hour we'll stick him on a state liquor law rap."

Brinkley put the bottle in his pocket, turned on his heel and went out. Some copper! He was small-town all right but he was sure tough. The clerk and the bell-hop went back to their places. I grinned at Shane and said:

"Kind of rough, wasn't he?"

Shane used a lot of words that the editor won't let me put down here.

I went back to the radio.

Shane got out a handkerchief and mopped some of the blood off his pug nose, and went over to the elevator and walked in. The bell-hop went in after him, pushed the door shut and the cage started up. This time I was sure it stopped at the fourth floor. It came back down and the shine came out of it and went down in the basement again and came up with another package just like the first and took it up to the fourth. The clerk didn't ever look up from what he was doing. When the shine came back down he sat down on the bench again and went to sleep with his chin hanging over on his chest.

Well, I got to thinking things over. Finally I decided it wouldn't do any harm to just go up and see him. So I turned off the radio and woke up the shine, and the shine ran me up to the fourth. He told me what room the guy was in too.

I knocked on the door and Shane opened it. He was still in his shirt sleeves, and he had a drink in his hand. He hadn't made any move to pack.

"Can I come in?" I asked him.

"Why not?" Shane stood aside.

I went in and closed the door. It was a little room with the bath built in on the left. Beyond that was the bed and on the right was the dresser. The bottle of liquor was on the dresser.

"Brinkley knows you got a car out back," I said. "You ain't going to take his advice?"

"Brinkley?" said Shane.

"The dick."

"Oh. That—" And he used some more of the words the editor won't let me put down.

While he was swearing I heard the elevator come up and stop and a moment later there was a knock on the door. Shane opened it. Brinkley stood there and ran his piggish little eyes over the room and saw that Shane hadn't made any move to pack. He came in and leaned against the bathroom wall and took out a gun and pointed it at Shane's belly. Then he said to me:

"I don't know what you're doing in here, buddy, but stay clear of this. I'm taking Shane in on the liquor rap."

I didn't say anything. Brinkley just knew me by sight. I'd been in town a week. I edged by him and put my hand on the door knob.

Shane picked up the bottle of liquor from the dresser. I turned the door knob, pulled the door inward an inch or two and then put some force behind it and slammed the door hard against Brinkley's outstretched gun arm. I couldn't see him then of course but I heard him gasp, heard the bottle smash and Shane had taken up his swearing right where he left off.

I closed the door and looked down. Brinkley was swaying there on his knees, his eyeballs all rolled up in his head. I could see blood trickling from the top of his head out of the bushy hair and running down in little streams by his ears on to his neck.

Shane stood holding half of the bottle. The other half lay in shattered pieces on the floor. There was liquor all mixed with the crimson on Brinkley's head and shoulders. The room reeked with the fumes of it.

Brinkley fell forward on his face, as limp as a dish rag. Of course we were in a spot but let me tell you I got a kick out of seeing him like that.

There are some coppers that you just can't help hating their guts and Brinkley was one of them.

"Let's get out of here," Shane said. "There's a fire escape at the back."

Never a peep out of him for giving him a chance to conk Brinkley. He just took it for granted. He went over to his bag, got out a shoulder holster with a gun in it, strapped it on, got some extra cartridges out of his bag and put them in a pants pocket, put on tie and coat and added: "I'll leave the rest of it. You got to go to your room?"

"No," I said. "There's nothing there to give me away. I've got my rod on me. My other stuff's in my car. It's parked at the back too."

"Yeah," Shane said. He leaned down and touched Brinkley's wrists, pried at Brinkley's eyeballs. He looked up at me with that ugly grin on his face. "This dick's dead."

I shrugged. "He asked for it. Let's go."

We went out, locked the door, and walked down the hall to a window. We climbed out of the window and went down the fire escape. There wasn't much moon and it was pretty dark outside.

"Follow me out of town," I told him when we started to split to go to our cars. "There's something I want to talk over with you."

He nodded and I went on to my car and started it up as quiet as I could and then ran off the ramp down to the back street and headed out of town. There wasn't a light to be seen anywhere the way I went. Not even a drug store or a café stayed open in that town all night.

I looked back every now and then and he was following me all right. Both of us had dark colored sedans of a popular make that aren't conspicuous. The fields were dark and ghostly and the big trees had this Spanish moss hanging all over them like they do in that country. It gives you the creeps if you aren't feeling just right, but I was feeling just right because I'd seen Brinkley get his, and there's nothing makes you feel better than to see a lousy copper get what's coming to him. Especially a small-town copper like Brinkley, trying to be so damned tough.

About ten miles out I slowed up until Shane was right behind me, and then I turned into a little lane underneath some trees that I knew about. There was a deserted farmhouse at the end of it, but I didn't go that far. I stopped under the trees and turned out my lights. It was dark then sure enough.

Shane pulled up behind me and cut off his lights too. He got out and came up and got in the car with me and lit a cigarette.

"I been here a week casing the lay for a bank job," I told him. "It'll be worth a hundred and twenty grand."

"Don't kid me," Shane said.

"I ain't kidding you. This is the tobacco season in this town and the bank's loaded with dough. They have what they call a tobacco market here, and the farmers all bring their tobacco in and get paid for it, and the bank has to have a lot of cash on hand."

"How do you know it's got a hundred and twenty grand?"

"We got some inside coöperation. The bank president's in on it. He can't lose because of the insurance. I've had everything fixed for a couple of days. It was supposed to be pulled day before yesterday but my pals didn't show up like they said they would. Last I heard of them they were in Asheville but I don't know where to get in touch with them there. And if the job ain't done today it'll be too late. This Davis, the bank president, says most of the dough is going to be moved today."

"How much of the take does Davis want?"

"He wants half of it, but hell!—we don't have to give it to him, do we? He's laying himself wide open and we'd be fools not to grab all we can."

I waited for Shane to say something to that, but he didn't say anything so I took it for granted he agreed and went on.

"We're supposed to go to his house and kidnap him and his wife and tie up his kids, and take him and his wife down to the bank with us about the time the time lock is ready to click. We have him with us so there won't be any monkey business about getting the safe open."

"Is it necessary to do it that way?"

"Sure it's necessary. It gives us protection in the first place, having him and his wife with us, and in the second place that's the way he wants it done—we got to string along with him. Then after we got the dough we take him and his wife with us a ways, put his wife out first, and then when we're far enough away to be safe, we give him his split and put him out. Only we won't give him his split. We'll just put him out. Oh, we can give him five grand maybe. He can't squawk!"

Well, there's no use to go over the rest of the conversation. We sat there and talked and planned things. He agreed to all of it of course. He'd have been a fool not to. It was a perfect lay except for what we'd done to Brinkley.

When his body was found they'd be on the lookout for us, but maybe his body wouldn't be found until after we'd got through at the bank. If it was and anybody spotted us—well, I had a Tommy gun under the back seat. We could blast our way out of anything that town could put up. . . . I admit I was a little scared, but hell!—we couldn't go away and leave a hundred and twenty grand laying there just waiting to be taken. It was worth the risk.

There was no state radio patrol—I'd never even seen any highway motorcycle cops. We planned what roads we'd take out of town, where we'd put Davis out, and everything else we could think of.

I had some liquor in the car and between the two of us I think we drank nearly a quart. I must have dozed off a while. When I woke up it was broad daylight—my watch said seven-thirty. I punched Shane and he sat up. We talked some more.

About eight o'clock we started back to town. We just left his car there. We wouldn't need it.

We were both hungry but there wasn't any use to run extra chances by stopping somewhere for breakfast. About half a mile this side of where we had been parked a fellow at a tourist camp stared at us as we went by, but I didn't worry about that because we had the Tommy gun ready and it wasn't likely the fellow had heard about Brinkley yet.

It was a pretty little town. You know, the kind that makes you feel like maybe it isn't so bad to settle down and get married and raise kids. It was a bright sunny morning and we were hungry as the devil.

The Davis house was a white bungalow with a hedge and a pretty green lawn in front. We parked and got out and walked up to the front door just as nonchalant as you please. There was nobody in sight.

A puppy on the porch saw us and started wagging his tail as hard as he could and put his dirty paws on my knees and wanted to play. I kicked him. He whimpered. The front door was open. We went in, taking out our guns. There was nobody in the living room.

I could smell bacon and eggs cooking. My stomach sort of turned upside down. I went down the hall to the kitchen while Shane went into a bedroom.

Mrs. Davis was a nice looking woman about thirty-five; plump, but not too plump. She had on an apron and she was cooking the bacon and eggs.

"Why Mr. Watkins—" she began. Watkins was the name I had used in this town, demonstrating vacuum cleaners. I had almost sold her one.

And then she saw the gun in my hand. Her eyes got wide and she stammered something, but I could see she still didn't quite understand just what the situation was.

"This is a stick-up," I said. "We're going to take your husband and you down to the bank and get the money. Nobody's going to be hurt if you do like I say."

She took a hand off the frying pan handle and sort of waved the hand around. She put down a fork she'd been using to turn the bacon. It was an electric stove.

"You better turn it off," I said. "It smells mighty good and I wish I had time to have some but you better turn it off."

She turned it off.

"Where's your husband?" I asked her.

"He—he's taking a bath."

"Let's go get him."

We went out of the kitchen to the bathroom and she knocked on the door. Her face was like a dirty sheet. I could see she wasn't in on the deal.

"What do you want?" Davis called.

I opened the door and went in. Davis was in the tub. He was a tall man with a wide mouth and hair that was beginning to turn gray. He braced himself with his hands on the sides and stood up in the tub, took one look at the gun in my hand and swallowed hard. "You—"

I nodded.

He got out of the tub and made a few nervous wipes with the towel, stuck his feet in slippers and pulled on a robe.

"We're taking you to the bank for the money," I said for the woman's benefit.

I herded them through an empty bedroom where Davis picked up his clothes and into another bedroom where Shane was with the two kids.

There was a boy about nine and a girl about fourteen. The boy was dressed but the girl was standing there in her pajamas trembling all over. She was a pretty little thing, too.

"Get dressed," I said to Davis.

I held the gun on them while Shane started tying up the boy and the girl and Davis dressed himself. Shane used a big roll of adhesive tape I had given him for the purpose. He put some across their mouths first and then taped their hands and legs to the bed. The girl was a little blonde with brown eyes. She certainly was pretty.

By the time Shane had them fixed, Davis was dressed.

"Take off your apron," I said to the woman.

She took it off. She had on a gingham dress.

Shane took a couple of pillow cases off the pillows on the bed, and when

I asked him what he was doing that for, he said: "We'll need something to put the money in."

I said, "All right," and to Davis: "Now you and your wife walk ahead of us out to the car. Our car in front. Try to act like nothing is wrong. If you don't act right you know what'll happen."

They did it all right and on the way out I told Davis to get in front with me and the woman in back with Shane. Davis walked very stiffly but I suppose he couldn't help it. After all, I don't suppose he'd ever done anything just like that before.

We all got in. Shane had his gun in his pocket, but when we got in he took it out and held it there loosely in his lap. We started off. Just as I was changing into high, a woman called out from the porch of the house next door. It nearly scared me silly. She was calling to Mrs. Davis, asking her something about where would the bridge club meet that day.

I said: "Answer her."

"At my house at two o'clock," Mrs. Davis called. It sounded pretty natural, too.

We drove on down to the bank. It was on a corner of Main Street. Some people looked at us and spoke to Davis and his wife, and they tried to nod or lift their hands as naturally as they could.

Shane put the gun back in his pocket and got out with Davis and the woman while I kept the car running. Shane had the pillow cases folded up in one hand. I could see Davis and his wife walk up to the counter ahead of Shane.

The cashier was standing behind the counter. I'd seen him before but he wasn't in on the deal. He said something and Davis said something back to him, and the man looked startled and put up his hands. Shane got them all at the back of the bank.

It seemed the cashier already had the vault open.

Shane stood with his back to the street so anybody that passed by wouldn't know he had a gun in his hand. Davis and the cashier started bringing money out of the vault and stuffing it into the pillow cases that Shane threw to them.

The whole thing didn't take but about four minutes. Two men went by but they didn't even look into the bank.

The cashier and Davis and the woman walked back out ahead of Shane and got in the car. Davis and the cashier were carrying the pillow cases stuffed with dough. Of course the cashier was afraid to try anything on account of the woman being in danger. Davis got in front with me and the woman and the cashier in the back. I didn't understand about the cashier.

"Why didn't you conk him and leave him under the counter?" I asked Shane.

"It's safer this way," Shane said. "We can put him out up the road. Let's go." He got in the back.

We went. Of course Shane kept the gun on them all the time. We passed by the hotel and there didn't seem to be any excitement there. As soon as we were out of town good, along a stretch where there were trees on both sides and no houses in sight, I stopped and told the woman to get out.

She got out and just stood there, her mouth quivering. Shane wanted to change places with me and drive, but I didn't pay any attention to him.

We drove on about five miles and

stopped again for the cashier to get out. He walked off down the road. This time Shane really put up an argument about driving the car. I couldn't understand it. He almost took the wheel away from me. I pulled my gun on him in spite of the fact that he had his in his hand. When I did that he got in the back of the car again, mumbling something.

I started to get some speed out of the car then. The more distance we got between us and that town, the better. The road wasn't paved but it was a good road. I got her up to seventy—eighty—ninety. We passed another car and a truck.

I could see Davis "putting on brakes" there beside me.

"Hey, not so fast!" Shane called. "There's no use attracting the attention of these cars we're passing!"

I didn't pay any attention to him. I kept her between eighty-five and ninety—that was about as fast as she would go. Shane kept yelling in my ear. I swore at him and told him to shut up.

We were about thirty miles away from that town when we got to the cross road where we were to put Davis out. There were a lot of high bushes growing at the intersection. Davis had a place he was going to cache his split there in the woods, I think. He was leaning back and arguing with Shane about his split. Shane had both the pillow cases on the back seat.

"You don't get a damned cent, Davis," I said, and stopped and opened the door for him to get out.

There was no one in sight on the cross road or on the highway either.

Davis called me a dirty double-crosser and some other things and I told him he was lucky to get off alive. What did he expect, anyhow? He knew he was mixing with tough customers to begin with.

"Aw, let's give him five grand," said Shane.

"To hell with him," I said. "He doesn't get a cent."

But Shane had counted out some money anyhow—five grand, I guess—and Davis got out of the car. Before I could do anything about it Davis had the money in his pockets—big bills—and was walking off toward the bushes.

"Come back here!" I called.

Davis didn't even look around. I called to him again and he started running.

I jerked out my gun and took a pot shot at him.

The slug hit him right square in the back and I saw him go over on his head like a rabbit before Shane's gun butt crashed against the back of my head and everything went black. . . .

WHEN I came to I was lying out on the road beside the car and Shane and Brinkley and three other coppers were standing over me. Davis was lying not far away. I could tell Davis was dead.

Of course it was pretty much of a shock—seeing Brinkley. I guess I must've gaped a little.

"You didn't croak him after all, Shane," was all I could think of to say.

"No, I didn't mean to," Shane said. "I'm an insurance dick."

"Insurance dick?" I mumbled.

"Sure," he said. "I hit town last night on my regular tour of inspection of banks. It was the first time I'd ever been here. I've been out in the Northwest a while. I recognized you in the lobby from having seen you in a line-up somewhere, and so

I called Brinkley and arranged for him to make the play in front of you, figuring you would crack to me."

"But Brinkley—"

"That stunt up in the room was all arranged. Brinkley stood backed up against the wall and I broke the bottle on the wall just over his head. He had a little rubber bag of red ink in his hair and we broke it so it looked like blood was running down on his head. I had blank cartridges too, but we didn't have to use them. You took my word that he was dead."

"Then—then you went through it all just to get Davis?"

"Had to, to get Davis. Brinkley and these other coppers been waiting here in the bushes. They heard our argument with Davis about the split and they were going to nab Davis with his share. That was why I wanted Davis to get some of the money."

"But how did they know—know we were going to let Davis out here?" he questioned.

"Remember when you fell asleep last night? I walked up to the tourist camp and called Brinkley. We had already planned everything. You didn't even know that I was gone for a while."

I got up on my knees, feeling shaky and trying to figure it all out. Finally everything clicked.

"It worked fine," Shane added, "except that you shot Davis before I could stop you. You get the murder rap."

That all happened about three months ago. I'm writing this in the death house of the state penitentiary. Tomorrow morning early they're going to walk me down that hall and put me in the chair and turn the juice on.

Wonder what Hell is like?

PLOW JOCKEY

By WILLIAM H. STUEBER

HE did not know that feminine eyes could be so stirring and magnetic. Nor did he realize that death lurked in those same limpid, sea-green pools set in the prettiest face he had ever seen. For a moment he was so enthralled that he forgot he was at a post office writing desk with his money order blank only half filled out.

Suddenly he remembered that a gentleman never stares at a lady. He shook off the spell, dropped his eyes, gripped his pen and scribbled hurriedly, then got on the tail end of the short line slowly filing by the money order clerk's window. But again some strange power turned his head; again his eyes met the magnetic orbs of the girl—and now her wistful smile drew ruby red lips and revealed teeth uncannily perfect and white.

He was the one man in a million who would not at once approach so dazzling and inviting a girl. Three weeks in the big burg were not enough to make him forget the things he had been taught back in Ringoes —where men respected women and a "pick-up" was unheard of. So again he looked away, knew he was blushing and fidgeting and wished to high heaven she'd go on about her business.

"Why elect me?" he asked himself. "Does she know I'm a hayseed? Does she think I've got a carpet bag full of greenbacks? Does she think it would be easy to clean my pockets or sell me Brooklyn Bridge?"

A hand resolutely touched his elbow. He was startled; then completely bewildered to find the girl beside him. He thought her short laugh the most musical thing he'd ever heard; her perfume sweeter than the scent of apple blossoms. He couldn't think that both were used deliberately—invitations to shake hands with death!

The girl pouted. "Are you high-hattin' somebody?"

"M-me? N-no, m'am. Not me. I —You must be mistaken, lady. You see, I'm—"

"For a week I've been tryin' to get a rise out of you. This is the first time I've met you where you can't run away." She laughed again; a laugh at once intended to make him less backward and to also tell the other gaping fools in the line to mind their own business. "Chickie's the name. My room is just across the hall from yours."

He blinked foolishly. "You mean you room at Mrs. McCall's?"

"Yeah! Didn't that old battle-axe tell you how anxious I was to know you better?" She was glad it was his turn to be served and nudged him toward the clerk's window and waited impatiently. "Hurry! Then we'll go some place and cry on each other's shoulder. Or don't you believe that this is a cruel, cruel world?"

In a few minutes he stuffed his money order into an envelope, ran the gummed flap over the tip of his tongue and dropped the letter into the chute for out of town mail. But there was nothing in his mind save the girl, and he readily confessed his pleasure at finding her to be no common flirt or street walker. He liked the way she clung to his arm as they walked to the street.

"That place you spoke about—"

"Nothin' classy," she interrupted quickly. "An' don't get the idea that I'm a gold digger. In fact, I'm payin' for you!"

His protests fell on deaf ears. He followed her into the cab that pulled up to the curb. In a jiffy he was in a part of town he had not yet explored and though again he protested, he paid the hackman with the greenback the girl thrust into his hand. Almost before he recovered his wits he was in a dimly lighted booth in a basement that had once been a protected speakeasy and was now called "Mickey's."

The girl grinned. "Unlax! Nothin' to be afraid of!"

"But—"

"You want to know what it's all about? Must I tell you anything more than that I'm also from the country —an' that this burg is the lonesomest place on earth for all its five million people? Do you follow me?"

He nodded. Sometimes during his three lonesome weeks he had felt on the verge of hiring some one to be a pal; sometimes he felt capable of listening to a lunatic's jabber. And here was friendship freely offered—he thought.

The girl planted both elbows on

the table, cupped her chain in two fragile hands. "Tell me about yourself," she practically begged.

The spirit of the occasion moved him. "I'm a better listener—anyhow, ladies first. Besides, it'll be more comforting if you talk."

A trace of a frown wrinkled her forehead. It instantly disappeared. "Country girl comes to seek fame and fortune in city. Saleslady in Jelkan and Moore's ; model in Goldstein's Cloak and Suit Corporation; two years in second rate vaudeville —and still a lonesome, friendless, jobless female. Dry, what? I'll bet *you* can tell things!"

"Some. And drier. I'd rather not. Let's talk about something else. How do you like this town of—"

"I hate this place," she said without venom. Then, seeing an opportunity to strike out directly toward her goal, she added languidly, "It's never given me the breaks—like you got. Mrs. McCall tells me you landed a good job the first day you arrived. Right?"

"Maybe I was lucky. Or maybe Mr. Laminson took me on because—" A waiter rigged out in pirate's garb came and took their orders for triple-decker sandwiches and tea. Chickie added a highball for herself, settled down in her chair and riveted her eyes on her find. There wasn't much information she needed to drag out of his reluctant mouth. For a week she'd been skillfully pumping Mrs. McCall. She knew his name was Gerald Cord—friends back in Ringoes had nicknamed him "Wheat." He was just another farm man, in the big town to try and rake up enough cash to bolster up the income from the old homestead. Mrs. McCall had said something about a loan for seed and a subsequent crop failure. Damned uninteresting, that! But when she heard that he was working for Laminson — chauffeuring the town's biggest banker . . .

"The trouble with working for a living here is that you get nowhere —an' use up a helluva lotta years doin' it," she said bitterly. "And working for the likes of Laminson is like selling your soul to the devil —for just enough to keep you in bread, socks and room rent."

Something happened to Wheat Cord. His face grew stern, his body rigid. "Mr. Laminson is a fine man. He's paying me more than I'm worth!"

"Oh yeah? Don't you know he couldn't hire any one else? Don't you know that his last chauffeur was murdered—and that unless you're wise, you might be next?" Her mouth curled with hatred. "I wouldn't work for Laminson for all the money in the mint."

"You wouldn't—"

"He's a skunk! Harvey was bumped off because he wouldn't fall in with some big shot crooks who wanted to rob the Laminson house. What did he get for sacrificing his life? Your boss had the murder hushed up—and Harvey's buried in Potter's Field!" She laughed derisively. "Honesty is the best policy! Go on *working* for a *living*. See how far you'll get in this man's town."

Wheat Cord studied her angry face. His own was gloomy. "You seem to know a lot about the Harvey murder," he said sourly. "And the truth is supposed to be a secret."

"Nothing is secret—if you're compelled to mix with guys in the know; guys who know more than the cops. Harvey—"

"Please let's not talk about that. I can see that you think Harvey was a fool. You think he should've betrayed Laminson—for a price, of course."

"Don't you?" she fired anxiously.

"No! Neither would I!"

His quiet words were reverent as an oath. They cut Chickie deeply. "You mean that if some one offered to give you a percentage of what they'd steal, for information you could easily supply, you'd turn the proposition down cold?"

"I would."

"Suppose that would be your death warrant?"

He looked her straight in the eye. "Don't think I'm playing hero when I say I'd rather die than bite the hand that's feeding me."

She leaned over the table and touched his hand. "Get wise, Wheat. Money makes the mare go. Do as everybody else does—get yours. The more you get the more people will respect you—and they'll never ask how . . ."

She clipped the sentence. It was plain that he was becoming angry. The waiter's arrival broke a half minute of strained silence. Chickie nibbled at her sandwich. Wheat pushed his aside untouched. His face was that of a pall bearer.

"I thought we were going to be great friends," he said morosely.

"Thought? Aren't we?"

"No. We're strangers again when we leave here. I'm no simpleton. Somebody ordered you to feel me out about doing what Harvey refused to do. You can tell them—"

"That isn't true!" she cut in hotly. Then an instant change came over her face, and tears in her eyes shone like fluid diamonds, to trickle slowly down her soft cheeks. "I—I just wanted to warn you. The men who killed Harvey will proposition you sooner or later. They'll kill you if you refuse to work with them."

He did not know that those tears could be turned on easily as a spigot. Believing he had come to false conclusions he promptly apologized. "But don't ever mention easy money to me again," he said smoothly. "And I wish you'd get such fool ideas out of your own head. Certainly you're old enough to know better and—"

She smiled for him. Never rush a prospect! Gradually she'd steer him in the right direction. No great rush! If she could get him completely in love with her he'd be easily handled. And by the very fact that he was not a sex-crazed man, she knew that her power over him—if once secured—would be the more absolute.

But when Chickie saw the last of him that night, she confessed that the first encounter had resulted in victory for him. She stood tensely inside the door of her room, heard a lock click across the hall. Frowning, she started to light a cigarette. Wheat had suggested she ought to stop smoking. She snuffed out the match and put down the fag, snatched it again defiantly, then shrugged her slender shoulders in surrender. Maybe he was right!

She paced the cramped room in a bitter mood, glared at herself in the mirror. "Sap! Letting a hick get under your skin like this!" she growled, throwing off her chic hat and fur trimmed coat. "You let Razz Adams get wind of your feelings and it's going to be just too damned bad!"

She flung herself on the bed trying to convince herself that after all Wheat Cord was only another man. But something about him had made an indelible impression; perhaps his countrified speech, his clean mind, his courage, or his very simplicity.

It was vastly annoying to find herself thinking more about a man than how she could make use of him. She spent some time trying to turn her mind to strictly business; so much time that with alarm she noted it was eleven o'clock—and she was due to report to Razz Adams at ten! She jumped from the bed, scrambled into hat and coat and hurriedly left the house.

The man she faced in suite ten-fourteen at the Van Dale Hotel was short of stature with long, gorilla arms that swung as he waddled about. His mouth, his eyes, marked him as a man of ruthlessness tinged with cowardice, and an air about him said that while he was prepared to bluff to attain his ends, he would also hammer and hack his way to them.

"Late!" he barked at Chickie as she followed the Jap servant into the luxurious living room. "An' your mug tells me you flopped!"

"I did," she snapped. "He's hard to get to. Took me a week to talk to him. He's straight, Razz; country straight—if you know what that means."

"Nerts! Smart enough to leave the country, means smart enough to grab dough when it's offered." He looked at her contemptuously. "Losing your charms or your grip? A week to see a guy—and let him kid you that he's straight?"

"But—"

"*I'll* see him. He'll come through or I'll fix his wagon!"

Chickie poured herself a drink at the buffet. She let it stand untouched. Wheat had suggested she drank too much. She turned slowly toward Razz.

"There must be another way to—"

"I told you a thousand times that the Laminson safe is guarded by the best alarm system that money could buy. It's fool-proof, unless somebody on the inside works with us. I need that combination. I need to know where the switches are. Even then it must be a daylight job—with a tip-off as to the proper time."

"Why can't you tackle something else? With Harvey bumped off, another killing of a Laminson chauffeur will set the whole burg on its ears and—"

"I've made up my mind to empty that crib. Get that? I'll do it if I have to knock over a dozen chauffeurs."

She shrugged her shoulders. "Your funeral. You'll proposition one chauffeur too many. He'll go to the front with the inside stuff. You'll fry. I'm telling you!"

Razz looked insulted. "Harvey was going to the front. Did I give him a permanent address? If this hayseed even suggests he'll spill the beans, I'll have him prepared for a hole beside the first fool. I'll see him. No more hints or beating about the bush. I'll tell him who I am, what's wanted—and what happens if he gives the wrong answers."

"That's playing tag with the hot squat!"

"Is it? Well, I'm marking the cards. I can't lose—much. That yokel does as I tell him to do!"

"And—and if he does?" asked Chickie thickly.

Razz gaped at her. "Are you cracked? If he does, you don't expect me to let him run around loose; maybe to talk or point his finger at me?"

She nodded gravely. "I see. Heads he loses; tails you win. Yes or no, he dies?"

"Safety first! A hick in the grave

is better than a hick shooting off his mouth at Headquarters or—" His mouth snapped closed. He took half a dozen rapid steps toward Chickie. His eyes flamed. To him, her face had always been as easily read as a book. Now he saw signs of rebellion. He gripped her arm, his finger nails digging into soft flesh.

She tore clear of his hand. "You let me—"

"So that's why you flopped!" he exploded. "He's put the Indian sign on you. You're goofy about him. You're—Get this, you fool! This job goes through. It goes through even if I have to bump off both of you. And it won't take me a helluva long time to find out where I stand with the boy friend."

He snatched his hat and almost ran from the suite. Chickie stood trembling, her eyes on the phone, her brain afire. She knew Razz Adams' methods. Once he suspected some one, he'd plug every avenue of escape and the moment his suspicions proved founded on fact, some one would die. Right now she visualized Razz rounding up his rod men and posting a detail to watch every move she or Wheat Cord made. She walked meditatively to the phone. She could ask Mrs. McCall to bring Wheat to the instrument in the lower hall. She could warn him that in short order his doom would be sealed. She picked up the receiver, choked on a sob and replaced it.

"He'll throw Razz out on his ear. He'll—he'll die before dawn," she told herself fearfully, pacing the suite like a caged animal. Then, exhausted and in black despair, she sank down upon the settee with fears all but strangling her. She knew now, the truth of the adage that she who longest derides love shall fall hardest.

But greatest torture she found in her knowledge that of her own free will—and with extreme pride—she had been first to discover Laminson's new chauffeur. And without orders or help from Razz, *she* had shadowed him, discovered where he roomed and then suggested that it was time to make a second effort to loot the safe. It was entirely her fault that Wheat Cord was in jeopardy; might even now be face to face with the ruthless man who never gave quarter.

RAIN lashed the windshield as Wheat drove through narrow, downtown streets the following morning. Lightning streaked across a sombre sky and in the gray semi-darkness all traffic moved cautiously. Wheat pulled up at the great bronze entrance to the bank and opened the Rolls-Royce door.

The shrewd-faced, elderly man in the rear compartment carefully folded his Wall Street Journal and agilely alighted. His hand clamped down on Wheat's shoulder and he smiled. "I didn't read a paper when you drove me down here the first few days," he said pleasantly. "And I'll forget my name before I forget how you sandwiched us between that coal truck and trolley car. Traffic nerves all cured?"

"Yes, sir."

"Anything *else* new?"

"No, sir."

"There will be! Sit tight." He took a step toward the bank, turned back, smiling. "And for pity's sake stop acting like a professional chauffeur."

"Y-yes, sir." Wheat saluted. "At four-thirty, sir?"

Laminson nodded and briskly entered the big banking house. Wheat drove off, west to Broadway and north to Murray Street. The powerful car no longer seemed like a hostile animal; the traffic no longer bothered him. In spite of the torrents of rain and the blinding flashes, he found he could drive and think of Chickie at the same time. Poor kid! Kicked around by fate and thrown into the company of roughnecks, yeggs and other assorted riff-raff. She deserved a break. Some day he'd ask her to be—

A short statured man stepped blindly from the curb. Wheat snapped on both sets of brakes, blew the Klaxon and kept his mouth tightly clamped lest his heart pop out of it. He knew the futility of hoping he wouldn't hit the jay-walker. In a split second the right front fender brushed against the short man who twisted and reeled backward with a shrill cry, then sat down in a mud puddle. Wheat came from behind the steering wheel as if hurled out by an explosion.

The victim sat moaning, massaging his scraped thigh and generally acting as if he were at death's door. Pulse pounding, Wheat helped two other men pick up the injured man. A crowd quickly gathered. Somebody suggested a quick run to the nearest drugstore; somebody else laughed hilariously and offered to be a faker's witness for half the pickings. An old lady elbowed up to Wheat and in no uncertain tone demanded that the groaning party be rushed to the nearest hospital.

Razz Adams decided he'd put on enough of a show. "I—I'm all right, young feller," he squeezed out. "Just take me home and we'll forget all about it."

He leaned heavily on Wheat and with difficulty made the car. Insisting on sitting beside the chauffeur, he grinned as the car pulled away just as a harness bull rounded the next corner.

"Now don't be so jittery," said Razz warmly. "Everything'll be okay. If you don't mind taking me home, you needn't even tell your boss about this."

"I've got to tell him," insisted Wheat. "Anything else wouldn't be fair or— Where do you live, mister?"

"Kingsbury. Thirty odd miles beyond city line. I'll direct you."

Wheat drove fast. In three quarters of an hour he found himself on a lonely, rutted dirt road. He thought nothing of the deserted aspects of the countryside. But when he was gruffly ordered to stop with no signs of habitation in sight, he sensed something unusual. And found it close at hand when he saw a gun in Razz's hand.

"This might be as far as you're going, Mr. Plow Jockey! Right here's where Chickie Vale's romance goes to hell—and maybe you, too."

Wheat's face went sour. "So, as I suspected, she was in cahoots with the men who killed Martin Harvey —and you're one of the same wolf pack?"

"I'm the kingfish, brother. The big shot, the main spring—and Chickie's been my best helper since I started as a two pint bootlegger. Thought her pure and simple, huh? Fell for her sob story about tough breaks? Got a lot of romantic bosh into your bean, hey? Well, maybe you're cured; maybe you can give some thought to *business?*"

"Maybe I will—if you give me an honest answer to just one question. Did she mix in your rotten business of her own accord or because you compelled her to do so?"

"She simply followed orders. Ditto

for you—unless you'd like to be stretched out beside Martin Harvey. Now let's get down to facts. The Bellfield National Bank is about ripe for a grand bust. Laminson knows that. He's feathered his nest for the flop. What's in that safe of his that it needs the greatest alarm system I've ever heard about?"

Wheat stared at him coldly. "Even if I knew I wouldn't tell you."

"Okay! But anyhow, you're going to get me the combination; the location of the master switch, and tip me off when there's fewest servants on duty. You'll get ten per cent of the take."

"Not for a hundred per cent and a bonus!"

Razz's laugh was short and deadly. "You're putting your John Henry on the dotted line of a death warrant."

"Think so?"

"I know so!" His gun hand tensed. "A promise to deliver the goods will net you one week of life."

"If I promised, I'd do it."

"I know you would. Meanwhile I'd have both you and the dame shadowed. Seven seconds after a hint of a double cross, you'd both die. Say no and you'll get yours right here; Chickie'll get hers as soon as I can reach a phone. You see, since last midnight, two of my men have been in the room next to hers at Mrs. McCall's—waiting for a phone call that means rub her out. So you've got two lives in the palm of your hand—and about three minutes to make up your mind."

It was like Wheat to think of himself last. Laminson, the folks back in Ringoes—and Chickie Vale flashed through his mind. The banker would only lose cash. The folks back home would lose their last straw of hope to keep from drowning in debts—and Chickie would lose her life. For even on his short acquaintance he realized that Razz Adams was desperately sincere in his threats.

"Well?" demanded Razz. His trigger finger was rigid, the gun leveled and steady. "Do you follow orders?"

Wheat sat tense as a tightly wound spring, his calm eyes on the weapon ready to spit death, his every nerve and muscle ready for action. "I do," he said sharp as gun cracks, "but not *yours!*"

Both his hands moved like striking snakes. His right smashed into Razz's face, his left seized the thirty-eight by the nickeled nose and wrenched it away. The effort was costly. Razz's finger convulsively jerked the trigger. The shot echoed across the deserted country and the bullet shattered the Rolls-Royce's windshield.

Fighting mad, elated by his success, Wheat brought the gun butt down on Razz's head with a vicious smack. But the would-be killer's hat softened the blow and he continued to yell with all his might while he struggled to open the door and flee. Wheat's second blow was a glancing one, for already panic-stricken Razz was half out of the car, faced to the rear and starting to run.

Wheat spun the weapon. A finger danced on the trigger as he leaped to the dirt road. Back toward him, still shouting for help, Razz pounded up the road. Wheat leveled his gun. It sagged. He could bring down a quail or pheasant on the wing—but he couldn't shoot an unarmed man in the back. He fired a warning shot over the fugitive's head and bolted after him.

A car swung crazily around a nearby curve in the cowpath. The moment he saw Razz swing to the running board, Wheat comprehended that it contained henchmen of the killer. Confirmation came instantly. Three guns barked spasmodically. Alive to his peril, Wheat dashed for the wheel of the Rolls-Royce with whistling lead lending wings to his feet. He started with the jerk of a racing motor and the gears meshed in high speed.

Lead whanged on the expensive body, spread fantastic cobwebs on the small rear window as wheels began to churn up mud. Hunched over the wheel, cold-nerved and determined, Wheat gradually got the accelerator down to the floor boards and breathed a prayer of hope for a road straight as the flight of an arrow. He tore along with split-second glances at the small mirror overhead and the grimness of his eyes and mouth faded as the gap between him and the pursuers grew longer and longer. Then, streaking up a long hill, he made a quick decision at a cross road, half skidded around a corner, shot down a twisting road and soon glimpsed smooth concrete straight ahead. He knew that precious few cars could overtake him now; knew he was safe—and that Chickie Vale was still in grave danger, for even now Razz Adams might be telephoning to his stationed killers, ordering the helpless girl butchered.

Wheat's head spun. He roared down the concrete, starving for sight of a gas station that boasted of a phone. Brakes screamed as he sighted one. He was out of the Rolls before the snapped back emergency brought the car to a halt. Minutes seemed centuries long as he waited for his number, and he prayed fervently against a "Line's busy" signal. The squeaky voice of Mrs. McCall quieted his fears.

"Ain't been a call since last Thursday," said the old woman. "Who? Yep. She's here. Hold on."

Another voice, oozing terror, reached him. "Wheat Cord," he said sharply. Words tumbled from his mouth with the speed of a machine gun's bullets. "No! *Don't* get the police! Stay in your room. Do as I told you. We mustn't frighten 'em away. I'll be there as fast as wheels can bring me."

He let her questions go unanswered, for he knew the value of seconds. Running out, he threw the station attendant a dollar, slid behind the wheel and drove off.

When the speedometer swung around to sixty-five, a hint of a smile curled the corners of his mouth. It looked as if a seed loan, some back taxes and a whole flock of long standing debts were going to be cleared up—at the expense of Razz Adams and his henchmen; looked as if they'd have plenty of time in which to remember a plow jockey.

RAZZ ADAMS gave vent to another sibilant oath as he dashed from a crossroads lunch wagon. He threw himself into the car, glared at four hard-boiled men and rasped a command for top speed.

"The damned phone's out of order," he growled. "If there's seventy an hour in this boiler, let's see you get it out!"

The parrot-beaked fellow behind the wheel crammed his heel on a muffler cut-out and stepped on the gas until the roar of the Buick's motor sounded like a plane in headlong flight. The speedometer read sixty-four. It wouldn't budge another fraction of an inch.

"Straight for hell," said one killer. "That's where we're headed for! The rube will get to Mrs. McCall's first. He'll get Chickie out of harm's way and have a flock of bulls ready to welcome us."

"Step on it," blasted Razz. Perspiration trickled down from both his temples. Though he reasoned the hick could prove nothing, he had a premonition that at Wheat's news the dicks would reopen the Harvey case —probably close it eventually with somebody in the hot squat. "If we're close enough behind him, he won't have time to arrange anything. We've got to get there first or right at his heels."

"That Rolls can do eighty without half trying," shouted the driver. "And look at this can! Steamin' already. Another five miles at this speed an' she'll fall apart."

Razz sat on the edge of the rear seat. The Buick made a sharp curve with one rear wheel leaving the road. There was a scream of tire as the chauffeur swung the vehicle back on the concrete to the accompaniment of the big shot's gasp of fright. Then with an exclamation half surprise, half delight, the driver slammed on all brakes.

Razz, too, let a wheeze escape his grim mouth. For not more than two hundred yards ahead stood the Rolls-Royce—with a state trooper's motorcycle propped up beside it and the light blue uniformed man writing on a pad he rested on the motor hood.

"Get going," cried Razz in high glee. "Now we've got him licked!"

The Buick went by trooper and Rolls-Royce at a respectable speed. But once out of sight of the officer, Razz himself took the wheel, swung into a rougher yet shorter route to the big town. Mouth clamped, eyes hopeful, he drove more recklessly than his chauffeur.

"Get there first!" he muttered. "When he arrives, let him have it—no questions asked. And don't forget to fix Chickie!"

He crossed the city line, jumped red traffic lights with immunity and parked around the corner from the rooming house. Every nerve on edge, he crouched against a drug store window and cautiously studied the brownstone front of Mrs. McCall's. He saw nothing promising disaster.

"Get in, Barlow," he commanded a shifty-eyed man at his elbow. "Keep the old woman out of sight. If she spots me the jig's up. She's known me since school days. She wouldn't know you from Adam. Work fast. Crack her on the head if necessary. Leave the front door unlocked. We'll be three minutes behind you."

"Okay! If I see anything screwy I'll be right out."

Razz gave his advance agent an extra minute. A vicious leer twisted his mouth. Coast clear! He nodded to his other men and started around the corner.

"And in spite of that damned plow jockey, I *will* empty the Laminson crib—some day!" he promised himself.

THERE was the hair-triggered tension of death in the top floor room at the rear of the semi-dark hallway. Wheat Cord stood against the closed door, Razz Adams' gun in one hand, a silenced weapon in the other. Two men squirmed as if their chairs were uncomfortably hot. On the table near the window lay two more silenced rods. Chickie Vale, remarkably cool, stepped from behind the prisoners.

"Okay, Wheat. Nothing else dangerous on 'em. What next?"

"Gag 'em. Get that rope off the

fire escape. Tie 'em up—good, and quickly. I don't think that trooper's escort to the city line brought me here more than ten minutes faster than Razz could make the trip, though we did touch eighty on two stretches of level road."

One of the prisoners screwed up his courage. "If that phone—"

"It won't ring," grinned Chickie as she laced the fellow to the chair. "You didn't get your orders because Wheat told me to cut the wires."

"And so Mr. Adams will come here to give the business his personal attention—I hope!"

"I'm givin' you plenty credit for crust," admitted the other gorilla. "Any other guy would have had half the police department here before he entered the house."

Wheat's face remained blank. "So would I—but my job says I get the Harvey killers *without help;* preferably alive, and yet without fear of the law if I'm compelled to take any one dead. There's a few other things you can tell Mr. Adams—before all of you go to the chair. Laminson's safe contains nothing but some antique silver heirlooms and a great collection of stamps which you couldn't sell for a dime because he'd immediately publish a warning and a list if they were stolen. Nor is the Bellfield National Bank ready to bust. Nor is Harvey buried in Potter's Field. Outside of that, your boss had everything straight—maybe."

"And you—"

Chickie's gag cut off the fellow's words. "You've said your last mouthful—outside of the District Attorney's office."

"Me?" drawled Wheat. "Laminson was ready to post a large reward for delivery of the Harvey murderers. I made him a proposition—or rather I begged for a chance to earn half as much. If Adams obliges by coming here—"

He clipped the sentence. Stealthy footsteps sounded outside the unlocked door. Chickie too, heard. She sidled to the table near the window and picked up a silenced gun. Wheat's previous orders had been to get out of harm's way. She couldn't see why she should obey. She flattened herself against the wall on the opposite side of the door and winked at Wheat as the brown knob began to turn slowly.

"Steady!" she said in a hushed whisper. "They've got to come in to see what's over in that corner. The lot of Razz's gunmen are yellow as ripe bananas. You'll—"

The door inched open. Then swung wide. Three men edged in cautiously. Drawn shades made the room even darker than the hall. They still peered about when Razz Adams stepped over the threshold. Like the others, he wasted no glances on what was *behind* him. Then in the same heart beat all the latest arrivals saw two men trussed in chairs.

Razz spun with a squeal. His hand darted for a heavy pocket. Chickie's silenced gun popped. The big shot's cry was of stark terror though the bullet only grazed the hairy back of his hand.

"Hoist 'em! Quick. All of you!" exploded the girl. "You might duck the hot squat with the help of some shyster lawyers. You won't duck slugs."

Good counsel! Razz was first to get his paws up. Only one man rebelled. He reconsidered when Wheat's trigger was on the verge of tripping a gun hammer.

"I'll run and get the harness bull on the beat to—"

"Empty their pockets first," cautioned Wheat. "And *don't* go out. Just open the window and yell—because there's one man missing. Probably on guard at the door downstairs."

There was no warning; no announcement that death lurked at the head of the stairs behind Wheat's back. The first intimation that Barlow had found it necessary to gag and lock Mrs. McCall in a downstairs closet, before he climbed to the top floor to see how the others were faring, came when his face showed level with the top floor landing—and his gun hurled a bullet at Wheat's back.

The missile skimmed a rib. Wheat whirled, teeth clenched against pain. He fired once. There was no cry; only the thump of a corpse bouncing down the steep flight of stairs.

Wheat steadied himself against the door jam. "N-now you can phone the nearest precinct, Chickie. And—and call Laminson at the Bellfield National. Tell him—the—job's done. And I'd like the five thousand—in small bills."

She looked at him morosely. Then, in a voice she tried to make hard-boiled, she asked, "You're going back home—right away?"

"I am. There's a train at six-twenty. Maybe you could go get me *two* tickets? Maybe you'd—you'd meet me at the gate?"

"Maybe?" Tears filled her eyes though she smiled. "Six-twenty? That's one train I won't miss. Bank on it!"

She ran out. No need to warn Wheat to be careful of his charges. Both his trigger fingers were tense.

The HEAT *for* CROSSERS

By CARL BERNARD OGILVIE

CHAPTER I

"Uncle" Schulzer

A THICK, murky fog hung in a depressive sodden blanket over Looptown. The heavy mist, greyed by sooty coal smoke, made a freakish night of the morning. A corner store clock, unseen, boomed nine.

One bright spot glowing in the mist, in a certain dismal North Clark Street block, was "Uncle" Dave Schulzer's shop window. Its border of bright lights cut a weird rectangular swath through the fog to the wet sidewalk, stabbed the mist upward to reflect on the trio of golden globes festooned from the lintel of a wide window. Those gilded globes announced mutely their ancient symbolism:

Enter broke; depart with cash.

Through the swath of light cutting the fog, figures of people going about their appointed daily tasks drifted. Suddenly out of the murk they loomed into light. Like ghosts from another world returning to haunt the money lender, known to the denizens of the underworld as "Uncle" Dave. Their brief phantom-like picketing done they evaporated into the fog, eerily, mysteriously, and as suddenly as they had appeared. Trolley cars rolled by slowly, bells clanging along the fog-bound street.

A tall reedy young man, grim face bent against the drizzle, approached the pawn shop slowly, cautiously. Snap brim pulled low down over his face, hands thrust deep into topcoat pockets, he paused, flattened against an adjoining building. Casting a hurried searching glance up and down the gloomy street, he suddenly moved to the plate glass door and was in Dave Schulzer's pawn shop.

He had not seen a thick-set man across the street, loitering in the protective shadows of a hall doorway. Private detective Charles Devon, working for a burglary insurance company client, had reasons for being there. He had strange ideas about Uncle Dave Schulzer. Ideas that Uncle Dave might be something of an undercover king-pin of the underworld. Ideas that he might be fencing a lot of "hot" stuff. Shrewd old Schulzer drove a hard bargain. An examination of his books had revealed only the prosaic day-by-day transactions of a small pawn shop. That the shop was a blind Devon had reasons to want to prove. Then he could cash in on the heavy rewards for a dozen recent jewelry-mystery jobs offered by his insurance company client.

Devon had fallen for the charms of Neva Schulzer, the pawnbroker's beautiful niece. She had turned him down flat in favor of Treve Kren, gem hoister and gunman. Kren wasn't the usual thickheaded rod. He had brains, knew how to use them. A dangerous man, Kren. But Devon figured that, with Neva's brother Benny nabbed the night before in multi-millionaire Horace Brewster's Gold Coast mansion, and seeing Treve Kren at this moment entering the pawn shop, he was about to get somewhere *fast.*

"'LO, Sweetheart," said Treve Kren as he entered the pawn shop, his wide mouth spread in a pleasant smile. He removed his snap brim, flicking beads of moisture from it, and moved toward the glass show case sparkling with jewels.

Behind the case was a slender, oval-faced girl with maddening large dark eyes set in a beautifully molded face. She looked up at him from a tray of diamond rings she was arranging. Bright overhead lights shimmered, danced in a glory of blue highlights on her glossy raven tresses. Some mental tenseness had drained some of the color from her smooth olive-skinned face. Her bee-stung red lips, languorous-lidded brown eyes were those of a woman who could love passionately or hate with a feminine, tigerish fierceness. Yet, even slightly pale, she was a striking picture of lovely, radiant young womanhood.

Neva Schulzer eyed the tall young man in natty tweeds. There was no feminine appraisal of his broad-shouldered, fine athletic-built body, his ruddy, handsome face, or the wavy brown hair that tumbled unruly over a wide forehead. She had done that many times before. It always set her heart pounding, warmed her blood. She shot a swift, apprehensive glance in the direction of her Uncle Dave busy at the safe in the rear of the shop. In a low voice that tugged at the muscles of her smooth throat she asked Kren:

"W-where's Benny?"

The huskiness of her voice, the apprehension flooding her eyes stirred Treve Kren strangely. He decided to pass off the jam her brother was in as lightly as he could.

He tried to smile reassuringly. "I'll have him here soon as Uncle puts up for Benny's bail bond."

A frown scarred the olive skin of her forehead. "He won't! Uncle's furious. He warned Benny to keep away from gangs," she whispered. "He's afraid to do anything for Benny because—"

"He's got to!" clipped Kren softly. "We pulled the Brewster job last night. Benny lost his head, plugged the butler. He'll pull through though, but Benny's charged with a list long as your arm."

"Vhat's this? Vhat's this?" A slight, short little man moved forward behind the show case. His greyish, bewhiskered face was thrust forward pugnaciously. He glared over the counter at Kren through heavy-lensed glasses. Iron-grey hair bushed beneath the little man's skull cap. In shirt sleeves and vest he was the characteristic "Uncle Dave" as always seen by high and low underworld characters.

Treve Kren said: "Dave, your nephew Benny is in a jam. Doesn't want you to know about it. I went to "Bull" Wilko, the professional bondsman and racketeer. He's got a mad on with you over something. Said he wouldn't bail a relative of yours out if he rotted in the can. So I had to come to you. Five grand ought to get Benny out. How 'bout it?"

At the mention of Bull Wilko the little man's face went hard. White bony fingers drummed on the glass counter top. His words were a hiss.

"Dot gonnif! After all I haf done for him. Made him a rich—" Schulzer cut off bitter words, pounded clenched fists against his flat chest. With challenging eyes he said, suddenly: "You made *mein* nephew a criminal. You swine! How did you get avay?"

Kren said: "I was lookout at the side drive entrance to the Brewster home. Benny was inside, upstairs. Working on the safe where Brewster's wife keeps her jewels. "Dog-Face" Bozan was in a hot car parked out front, watching the boulevard. All of a sudden he beats it. A squad car races into the drive. I beat it into the house by the rear door, gave Benny the signal to take it on the lam. He ran down the front stairs. The butler got in his way. Benny lost his head and dropped him with a shot in his leg. Then the kid ran kerplunk into that private dick Devon's arms. He had the cops with him. I beat it over the back fence, got away. It wasn't the cops' fault; they tried hard enough to plug me."

"So—" The little man seemed to age as Kren talked.

Neva gasped in anxiety: "Treve, you're in danger of being picked up any minute. The cops might have recognized you!"

Treve Kren jerked up his face. "The cops only saw my back; it was too dark."

He took a newspaper from his top-coat pocket, spread it over the case. "Lookit. Picture of Mr. and Mrs. Brewster at the opera last night. Wearing her famous pearl necklace. Dave, we were crossed on this job. The tip was Benny would find the necklace in the safe. Why were we sent there the very night the dame was wearing them to see *Cavaliers Rush-the-cana?* How did the cops know *exactly* what time to barge in? It's a dirty cross. I mean to get Benny out of the coop. We'll get the rat that squealed on us. Who knew about this besides you?"

Uncle Schulzer's eyes grew small behind the thick lenses. "I von't gif you money for dot kind of pizzness. I am an honest man. I do an honest pizzness."

"You're breaking my heart, you foxy fence," rapped Kren. "Dog Face Bozan hired Benny and me to do the job—then ran out on us. Rat! I know you don't like me because I make eyes at Neva. I'm nerts about her. An' I'm gonna marry her whether you like it or not. Now you like me less for getting Benny in with a mob. But get this, you hide-bound skinflint, you're forking over five grand so I can get your nephew out of the brig, and right away."

The guile in Uncle Schulzer's eyes was shielded by his thick glasses. To Uncle's crafty way of thinking, if he were to bail Benny out at once his act might, in the eyes of the police, be an admission of his complicity in the Brewster job. He said resignedly:

"If Benny is a crook, he must stand the consequences. I am an honest man."

Treve Kren knotted fists. His voice, raised in anger, drowned out the sound of the front door opening somewhat stealthily.

"I'm asking for Benny—your own flesh and blood. You fork over the cash or you'll wake up some morning and find your skull cap and what's beneath it bashed in."

"Tough egg!" clipped a cold voice at the other end of the shop.

Kren pivoted to stare into the level gaze of Private Detective Devon.

CHAPTER II

Treve Kren's Fadeout

AT sight of the private dick Uncle Dave Schulzer's heart was gripped by a convulsion of panic. He had fenced considerable hot stuff for underworld characters. He got rid of it promptly, made handsome profits. Dave, in fear that Devon had traced hot stuff through his shop, was panicky. The detective's sinister presence demanded strategy, Schulzer decided. He played a wild reckless bluff. In a voice pinched with pretended fright he screamed:

"Help! I'm being robbed!"

From a drawer beneath the counter he whipped out an old nickel-plated contraption resembling a revolver. Flourished it at Kren with a wavy hand. He even thought of carrying the bluff to the limit of shooting at Kren point blank—but aiming over his shoulder. But Uncle's terror of being exposed, however, did not stun a crafty quirk of his agile brain. The sound of shots would bring the police. He did not want policemen in his shop.

Devon's voice rang out sharply: "Put down that gun, Uncle!"

Schulzer did. Wiping beads of perspiration from his brow with the sleeve of his shirt he panted, his voice a thin cackle.

"You haf saved mein life. This low-lifer vas trying to rob me!"

"That's not so," gasped Neva, large eyes flashing fire.

"Shut up!" barked her uncle.

Kren, eyes cold, squared his shoulders, faced Devon. He regarded the snub-nosed detective-special low at Devon's side, pointed at him. Kren smile wryly, said in a tart tone:

"Got your nerve, barging in here

with a rod. What do you think you are, a cop?"

Devon made a sour face. "Any decent, self-respecting citizen would plug a mug like you caught holding up a shopkeeper." He put his revolver in his pocket, his right hand still gripping the butt. Devon turned his flat face toward Neva, asked in a voice intended to be soft:

"How about a little date—with me?"

Neva, her face a mask, answered, "Sure. When?"

"Eight-thirty, tonight."

"Oh," snapped the girl in mocking surprise, "I didn't know they held funerals at night."

Devon blanched. "I'll let that crack pass," he clipped.

Kren grated: "Put on your act, mug."

Devon moved up to him, said: "My client insured the Brewster gems. The Brewster mansion was entered and the butler got creased. The jewels are safe, but that don't lessen *my* interest. A long stretch is waiting for some mugs. The same gang that has pulled a dozen similar Gold Coast jobs the last few months. I mean to get 'em. My client has taken a heavy rap on the cuff. Kren, you were at the Brewster house last night."

"Who says I was?"

Devon eyed Kren's tan tweed topcoat.

"This."

The detective drew his left hand from his coat pocket. His fingers flexed open revealing a small object in the palm of his hand.

"Found it hanging on an iron paling of Brewster's backyard wall," Devon offered, smiling serenely with the air of a man putting over a master stroke.

Four pairs of eyes riveted questioningly on the object. Then, as if governed by an unseen power, four pairs of eyes simultaneously swept to Kren's topcoat. He swung half-around, his hand pawing at the coat's tail. Amazement swelled into all the eyes but those of Devon. In his hand was a jagged-edged piece of tan tweed cloth. About an inch square. In the skirt of Kren's topcoat, near the tail was a hole the size of that piece of tweed. It did not take an expert to see easily that the piece of material in Devon's hand would fit perfectly in the hole in Kren's coat. And Devon had said he found it sticking to an iron paling of Brewster's wall!

Kren, in a flash, recalled now the sharp tug on his coat as he leaped over the wall. That was when the coat had been torn. His mind, filled with thoughts about Benny, had failed to register the probable importance of the incident till this moment. That morning he had been in such a hurry to try to get Benny out of jail he had got into his coat without noticing the rent material. Kren knew now Devon had him in a tough spot.

Uncle Schulzer made strange clucking sounds through his teeth.

Neva gasped a deep-throated gasp of despair. She cried:

"It's a frame-up! Kren was with me last night. We went to McVicker's—"

"That's an old one, sister," Devon grinned. "I suppose you'll show me the ticket stubs."

"I—I—Kren—"

"Yeah? What show was on?" challenged Devon.

Neva couldn't answer.

Devon winked. "The eternal woman lying to save her man—"

Kren leaped, hands outstretched to grasp Devon's hand, tear the damaging evidence from him.

Devon's fists balled into hard knots. His left came up in a short uppercut that cracked on Kren's square jaw. Kren and Devon hated each other like two bulldogs. They tore savagely into one another, exchanging blow for blow. They were about the same weight—around one hundred sixty. Kren took a terrific wallop on the temple and felt his knees buckle under his weight. Head throbbing, he leaped at Devon, sent blows to body and face with sledge hammer force. Devon planted a searing uppercut to Kren's mid-section. But Kren continued to send blows into the private dick. Devon backed up; Kren measured him for a knockout.

Crack!

Devon's arms flung out, his head seemed to snap back between his shoulder blades. He crashed to the floor with the dead weight of a falling, unconscious man.

Kren stooped over to open Devon's knotted fist where the bit of coat material still reposed. Before he could get it the front door swung open. A blue uniform on a large solidly-built man filled the doorway. Captain Corran's authoritative voice rang out.

"What's going on here?"

Schulzer screamed like a frantic monkey: "Dot low-lifer Kren tried to rob me. He threatened to kill me! Den dot dick came in und saved me!"

"He looks like he didn't do so well for himself," muttered Corran.

Neva cried: "Quick Kren. A bull!" She ran to the end of the rear showcase. Deft fingers lifted her skirt revealing a snubbed-nosed automatic in a garter holster at the top of a slender, graceful, silk-stockinged leg.

THE warning note in her voice stirred Kren to instant action. He spun around, raced along the showcase. He whipped the automatic from Neva's garter-holster, barged to the back door of the shop.

"Stop!" shouted Captain Corran, plunging forward, hand reaching for his service revolver.

Kren flung the back door open. He slammed it shut behind him, barged across a small yard.

The form of Captain Corran bristled in the doorway. "Halt! I'll shoot!"

Kren plunged on—twenty feet ahead was the alley and its protective shadows hung deep with murky fog. Two shots rang out behind him as Corran fired into the fog. Kren heard the bullets slap into the brick wall as he rounded the corner of a building. He ran until he came out into a street.

Corran was in the alley but did not fire again. He was afraid he might shoot an unseen passerby in the fog that had swallowed up Kren.

Flagging a cruising Checker Cab, Kren got in, snapping an address.

Going back to the pawn shop Captain Corran heard Schulzer's story repeated. Devon gave the lowdown, as he had it, on Kren. The captain snapped:

"I'll get a rider out for Kren. Every squad car will be on the hunt for him until we get him."

Schulzer wailed: "Kren told me he vas the brains of dot Brewster job, Captain. He got mein poor Benny in bad."

Corran looked pleased. "You willing to swear to that?"

"Vhy not, Captain? Ain't I an honest man?"

CHAPTER III

Bull Wilko

A KEY grated in the lock of the door of Treve Kren's West Side one-room hideaway. He quickly moved to his dresser, hefted a flat automatic in his hand. The door opened. A form moved into the room.

Always smartly dressed, Neva came in wearing a sodden blue jacket and skirt. Her hat was wilted, her stockings and shoes were mud-splashed. Her eyes were round. Her face muscles were working strangely. She gasped:

"The police took Uncle to Headquarters for questioning. He'll lie you into jail." She closed the door.

Kren tossed curly brown hair out of his blue-black eyes, put his automatic back on the dresser. He moved to a stand table, picked up a cigarette case, offered her a pill. She refused and he lit one for himself.

"Well," she demanded. "What are you going to do about it? Just stand there and smoke?"

"You're soaked. Take off your things. Dry them over that radiator. Fall in the river?"

Neva's black eyes snapped. "No. I shut up shop after Uncle left with the police. I took a cab here. A car followed us. At Halsted I told the driver to try to get away from whoever was tailing me. He took the corner too sharp—the palooka! Skidded against the curb—broke a rear wheel. The other car disappeared. I stood there in the rain waving at passing taxis like the Statue of Liberty on the loose. Cars whizzed by and did they stop? They splashed mud all over my ankles."

Neva donned a bathrobe of Kren's, laid out her things to dry. She strode about with nervous energy, a slim, boyish figure in masculine garb.

"The cops have a rider out for you, Treve. This sure is a fine mess. God, Treve, we've got to get out of this life now, before it's too late. First it was Benny; then it'll be you. I'm so sick of this hellish existence, I can't stand it any longer." Her voice broke into rasping sobs.

Kren patted her on the back. "You'll be all right, kid. It's Benny that's got you. Forget it, now."

She eyed him coldly. "This isn't the first time I've felt this way, Treve. This is the end for us, I guess. You've got the brains, but you're in the wrong crowd—and I guess you're too weak. But I'm quitting as soon as we can clean this mess."

"You're not quitting me, Neva, not even if I have to get out of this to stick with you."

He sat down in an armchair. His movement about the apartment drowned out the sound of soft footfalls in the hallway outside.

"I've got a plan," said Neva grimly, "to square with Uncle and get Benny out of stir. He's an honest man, yeah! Well, listen. When papa and mama were killed in that auto accident ten years ago, papa left a will. We were to get fifty thousand dollars split between us when Benny became of age. Uncle, who lost his wife two years before, took Benny and me to live with him. As administrator of the estate he took the fifty G's which were in good sound bonds. Papa was a bootlegger, but he bought good bonds. I'm going to get those bonds to get Benny out on bail."

"How are you gonna do that?" Kren wanted to know. "I thought your uncle said he lost your money in the Dexter Bank crash."

"Yeah?" smiled Neva perching on

the arm of his chair. Her voice rose in her excitement. "That line about the bonds being lost in the crash is a stall. Benny was of age a year ago and he and I should have got them then. Uncle's stalling to keep us from getting our rightful dough."

"Have you proof?"

"Only this noon I wised up," went on Neva excitedly. "I was down in the store and heard Uncle upstairs in our apartment. I went up the back stairs and what do you think I saw? Uncle had the big cabinet radio pulled out from the wall. I saw a small safe built into the cabinet below the radio set. Uncle was looking at his radio chart that he logs the stations on while turning the dial of the safe. I thought he was nerts. But the safe opened and I saw him check over a lot of bonds. I beat it before he saw me. After Uncle left with the cops I locked up and went upstairs. What do you think I found? Well, listed as station G E L T was the combination of the safe. Clever old Uncle! He don't use the safe much and so he keeps the combination handy in case he should forget the numbers. I've seen it dozens of times but never tumbled that *gelt* is German for gold."

"You got your bonds?" breathed Kren, suppressing his excitement.

Neva shook her head negatively. "I'm not putting my fingerprints on any safe. Uncle would murder me. But here's my plan—"

She cut her words short, shot a glance of alarm at the door. She whispered: "Maybe it's the mugs that were following me."

Neva got up, wrapping the robe tightly about her slender curved body.

Kren moved to the dresser where he had laid his automatic. Leaning there he jerked his head for Neva to open the door.

She moved to it. Putting her ear to it she listened intently. She turned away with a shrug of her shoulders.

"Someone going down the corridor." She moved over and sat on the bed to the right of the door. The robe splayed open and her body glowed like a bronzed statue. "Now this is how we'll work it, Kren. Uncle is nerts over the food served at the Viennese Café. Likes to go there and listen to the Viennese orchestra—sits there for hours. Now, I'll get him to take me there tonight, right after we close shop at nine. While we're away, Kren, you'll slip up the back stairs to the apartment. I'll give you a key. You'll find the safe combination on the radio card, get the bonds. Bring them here and I'll come get them and give you enough to bail Benny out. I've got to get that kid out."

"Sounds like a cinch," said Kren. "I'll do it for you and Benny. If Uncle has crossed you, he's got the cross coming back to him."

The door bell jangled petulantly. Kren moved to the dresser to be near his automatic. Neva opened the door.

Two hard-faced men crowded into the room. One was slender with an ugly mouth like that of a bull dog. Dog-Face Bozan held a vicious looking automatic in his gun hand. The other man was big, beefy, swarthy—Bull Wilko, professional bondsman and political boss of his ward. He eyed Neva in the robe that had slipped off one shoulder revealing the loveliness of her shoulder and throat. His eyes lit up with strange flames.

"Sorry to bust in on this," he leered.

"It ain't what you think it is, Wilko," snapped Neva. "What you tailing me for? I'll bet you were the mugs following me in that taxi."

Wilko shrugged, pushed back a mop of hair out of his small black eyes.

Dog-Face Bozan clipped, automatic prominent as it leveled at Kren: "Keep your mitts in sight! There's somethin' screwy 'bout last night. You gettin' away an' lettin' Benny get collared. I got away clean an' I'm stayin' clean. Get this, Kren, I got a hunch you tipped the job. I'm in no mood to argue."

Kren grated: "That goes for me too. I'm thinking things about *you* that ain't so good."

Wilko shot a swift glance at Bozan, ordered him to put his gun away and shut up. Wilko said:

"Kren, Dog-Face was spottin' Uncle's shop since dinner. He sez the bulls got him. What's the lay?"

"Worried?" Kren asked with a sly grin.

Wilko shrugged beefy shoulders. "You know how it is. Uncle an' I used to do a lot of business together. I thought mebbe he might be sore 'cause I didn't bail the kid out. I've hired Dog-Face to be my guardian angel till things clear up."

Neva flashed angrily: "You're going to put up the money and bail Benny out of stir tonight."

"Who sez so?"

"I do. I'm not asking favors of your kind," said Neva, her brown eyes smoldering. "Before midnight Kren will bring you five G's worth in good bonds."

"Yeah? Where's he gonna get 'em? I'm not sap enough to get caught with stolen securities."

"They're mine," said Neva. "He's going to take them—"

Kren cut her off short.

"Never mind the details. You want security for your cash, Wilko. Well, we're gettin' it for you. I'll be round to your dump with the bonds. You can get papers made out for the release. Or you can have Benny sprung on my word you'll get five G's in bonds tonight."

Wilko's eyes flashed some incomprehensible message to Dog-Face. Kren didn't like it. He shot a glance at Dog-Face. Treacherous flames glowed in the gangster's eyes. Kren's heart went chilly. How long had they been in the hall outside his door? Had they overhead the very complete step-by-step of Neva's plan?

Wilko stuck a fat cigar between thick red lips. "Better make it ten G's for a safe margin."

He touched a match to the cigar. An unnatural dreamy glow came into his flinty eyes.

Dog-Face's voice was a growl. "Bring along an extra G for me—if you want me to keep my mouth shut. I'll scram outa town for a while."

"Chiseler!" rapped Kren. "I have a hunch, Dog-Face, you'll leave town in a box."

Dog-Face jerked his homely face down on his chest, rolled flinty eyes. "You'll be so far under you won't know about it."

Wilko and Dog-Face helped themselves to swigs from a bottle of Kren's rye and moved to the door. Wilko said to the girl:

"I'll play with you, baby. See you later Kren—"

After they had left Neva noticed the black frown on Kren's face.

"What's the matter, dear?"

"Nothing." He didn't want to perturb her unnecessarily. But if Wilko and Dog-Face had heard her plans it meant they would have the bond job on him. That wasn't so good. That would make three that had something on him. Devon still had that damned piece torn from his topcoat!

A dreamy, yearning gaze had come into Neva's languorous eyes. For a moment she sat moodily, gazing into blank space. Then she pulled herself together.

"Everything is going to work out all right," she whispered.

Kren was frowning as he kissed her. He wasn't so sure. He felt worried—damned worried. A keenly developed instinct told him something wasn't going right. Well, he'd hope for the best.

CHAPTER IV

Murder

TREVE KREN, in a northbound street car, studied Schulzer's pawn shop as the trolley rumbled past. The customary brilliance of the windows was darkened now. Only a light glowed in the rear of the store over the big safe.

Try as he might Treve Kren was unable to shake off an indefinable sense of uneasiness, a feeling of foreboding of some terrible menace hovering over his head. He didn't like the job of robbing Schulzer. Yet the old buzzard had no sentimental feeling for Benny. And it was Benny Kren wanted to help. After all he wasn't really going to rob Schulzer. The bonds in his apartment safe legally belonged to Benny and Neva. Benny had to be sprung. Together they could ferret out the rat that had tipped off Devon or the cops to the Brewster job fluke.

With the coming of night a fresh spring breeze had swept in off the lake. It had rolled the fog away. Street lights glowed brightly in a steady light rain.

Kren got off the trolley at the corner. He glanced down Clark Street to Schulzer's darkened shop. It was nine twenty-five. Suddenly his pulse quickened. He saw a girl come running out of the shop. She was carrying a dark object under her arm—a bundle or a large sized pocket book. She flagged a taxicab and got in. Neva. And she was supposed to be at the Viennese Café with Uncle Dave. Kren moved to the curb to flag the cab, call to Neva. But the taxi whirled around in the middle of the block and churned away in the opposite direction.

Puzzled, Kren long-legged to the alley, approached the pawn shop from the rear. He went up a straight flight of rickety wooden stairs to an enclosed storm porch. He went in. Putting the key Neva had given him into the back door lock, he turned it slowly. He moved the door in. Listened. Inside the little six-room apartment was deadly quiet. Dark. Kren moved into the kitchen. In the dining room a great grandfather clock ticked loudly, with solemn, mechanical precision.

Tick—tock.

Kren, flashlight in hand, went toward the living room.

The clock's solemn ticking jangled in his ears, made his nerves jump.

Tick—tock—tick—tock.

The old clock seemed to be ticking some mournful warning, communicating to him in its eery, steady, ticking:

Go—back. Go—back!

Kren had been to the apartment several times. He knew his way about. Off the living room, beyond velvet portières, was a short hallway. There were the bedrooms and bath. Uncle's bedroom first, then Neva's. Both faced the street. Benny's was on the side next to the bathroom. The living-room was vaguely lighted by the reflection of street lights sending their glow in through lace-curtained windows. The dismal, haunting stillness of the darkened rooms tautened Kren's nerves. He had a strange disturbing feeling that he was not alone in the apartment. He felt as a ghoul must feel stealing into a cemetery vault to rob the dead.

Suddenly a blinding blue flame blazed through the living-room, filling it completely for an instant with a freakish light. The blinding flash was followed by a crackling sound.

Kren's left arm swung up involuntarily to shield his eyes. His right had flashed to an armpit holster. He waited breathlessly in the gloomy shadowed room.

A street car rumbled along the tracks outside. Then Kren knew the flash of flame had been caused by the trolley slipping off the wet high-tension wire. He cursed his jangling nerves, tried to smile. Couldn't.

That clock! With each swaying of the pendulum its irritating ticking seemed to say now:

Death-death. Death—death—

As if to dissolve the ghastly hush hanging over the apartment, Kren thumbed on the light switch. The overhead chandelier stabbed the darkness with light. A low moan wrenched from Kren's clenched teeth.

The radio cabinet had been pulled out from the right hand wall. There was the safe, its door open. Not believing what his eyes already told him, Kren bounded to the cabinet, ran his hand into the safe. Empty!

He spun around, brain crowded with tumultuous thoughts. It was then he noticed the velvet portières, that had always hung over the doorway leading to the bedroom hallway, lay in a jumbled snarl on the floor.

Kren leaped over the portiéres, caught himself up short. By the diffused light stealing into the first bedroom from the street window and the lights of the living room, Kren made out the shadowy form of a body. It lay on the bed. Feet sprawled apart, torso hanging over the side of the small bed, head down, arms dangling until the hands touched the floor, it presented a ghastly spectacle.

Kren pushed the light switch on.

"Dave!" gasped Kren in round-eyed amazement.

TREVE KREN lifted the little man by the shoulders, placed him on his back on the bed. The bed clothing was disheveled, showing signs of a struggle. Kren picked Schulzer's glasses from the floor. On a stand table beside the bed he placed them near a half-empty water glass. Next to it was a bottle of veronal tablets. He felt the old man's pulse and heart. The body was still slightly warm. There wasn't the faintest trace of heart action. He took a hand mirror from the dresser, held it before the gaping mouth. No mist showed on the mirror. Schulzer was dead.

Then Kren noticed the strained, set expression on the man's face. The muscles were set in a terrifying expression of unutterable horror. In terror, struggling for his life, Uncle Dave Schulzer had died.

Kren unbuttoned the torn jacket of Schulzer's pajamas. So interested was he in making a cursory examination for a wound that would tell him how Dave had died, Kren failed to hear the faint tread of footfalls mounting the back stairs.

"Overdose of veronal," Kren decided aloud to himself.

"Sez you!" rapped a sarcastic voice from the living room.

Kren pivoted. Standing in the other room, where at an angle he could look into the bedroom, stood private detective Devon, gun in hand, ready for action.

Devon sneered. "Looks like I got you in pretty deep muck this time, Kren. Too deep for me. I'll have to call Cap Corran in. Murder is out of my line. Don't seem to be with you."

CHAPTER V

Life-Saver

"YOU sap! There's not a wound on him," blurted Kren. "He musta took too many of those sleeping tablets. You're a sap if you think—"

"Naw. It's my gold tooth that makes me look that way," sneered Devon. He moved to the bed, gun leveled at Kren.

"Nice set-up. Perfect. Too perfect," sighed Devon in a knowing, irritating manner. "Don't know if you could jam an overdose of those pills down a dead man's throat or not so the docs would find the dope in his gizzard. Might at that, after choking him to death—while the throat muscles were still wrenching."

"What you talking about?" demanded Kren.

"Those purple marks on his throat," smiled Devon with a superior air. "Don't tell me those are liver blotches. They're fingerprints. The stiff was choked to death."

Kren swept a swift glance at the dead body. The light at the head of the bed had shaded the dead man's throat and Kren had not noticed the telltale marks.

Devon said: "I've been hanging around outside. I saw the lights go on up here so I dropped in. Social call."

"Cut the comedy."

"It all fits. The cops questioned the stiff this afternoon," said Devon. "He didn't spill. But he got a good scare rammed in him. Brewster wouldn't push the charges because Benny is still a youngster, twenty-two. Besides the job was a fluke and Brewster's butler is on the mend. This morning I heard you threaten to get Uncle. Neat job. Might even have got away with it if I hadn't spoiled your play. But there's one or two things I don't get— You know that the cops turned the kid loose 'bout an hour ago? I was there when he got out. He was madder than a riled serpent. Said he'd tell his old tight-fisted uncle a thing or two. There was blood in his eyes—"

"Then Wilko *didn't* bail Benny out?" Kren asked.

Devon's eyes grew small. "That's a thought. I've had that racketeer on my list for a long time. You guys hoisted the hot stuff, Uncle fenced it and Wilko bailed your boy friend out. Swell combination. No wonder I haven't been getting anywhere. But you can bet I got you."

Hurried footsteps sounded on the front stairs. Someone bolted into the living room. Devon turned his head to see who had come into the apartment. That was his mistake.

Crack!

Kren's knotted fist caught the private dick squarely on the jaw, grabbed his gun wrist. The dick seemed about to go down. Kren yanked Devon's gun from his hand, tossed it out of reach on the bed. He pushed the dick out into the living room.

"Neva!"

The girl surveyed the two men with wide eyes. "What's happened?"

"Nothing, only this dick likes to push his puss in places at the wrong time. I just pushed it out."

Devon sank into a chair rubbing his throbbing jaw.

Kren, moving out of the hallway, stooped, picked up the portières. His eyes riveted on an oval metal object. A brooch caught in the portières. His hand closed over the bit of novelty jewelry. His eyes flashed to Neva. At the V neckline of her blouse he detected a small hole.

"What you got there?" Devon demanded, sitting up slightly.

"Nothing."

Maddening thoughts pounded in Kren's whirling brain. He had seen Neva hurry into a taxicab. Her brooch must have caught on the portières, tore the pole supporting them from its fastening. Neva! Kren couldn't get the terrible accusation out of his mind. She had drugged her uncle. She was big enough, strong enough to choke the little doped man to death.

Kren's face went hard. He moved over, stood in front of Devon.

"You got me cold, Devon."

Devon looked up suspiciously. "You're a cool number, Kren. You're hard. I didn't think you'd admit it without a workout at Headquarters. Give me your gat."

Kren took a flat automatic from his shoulder holster, handed it to Devon, butt first.

NEVA ran into the bedroom. No scream came from her lips, no sobs. This told Kren that she was neither surprised nor grief-stricken at seeing the body of Schulzer.

Devon said: "I have no authority to arrest you. This is a criminal case. But I'll be the star witness that will send you to the hot squat."

Kren answered in a spiritless, heavy voice:

"I know when I'm caught cold."

"I'll call the cops," decided Devon. He moved to the telephone, picked it up. Jangling the hook impatiently his eyes ran along the wires. "Cut! You think of everything, Kren."

"Yeah," retorted Kren gloomily, eyeing Neva as she came back into the room. Her right hand hung at her side, hiding behind her thigh Devon's revolver she had taken from the bed.

She squared her shoulders bravely, said:

"I—I wished I hadn't—"

"She don't know what she's saying," cut in Kren.

"I do," wailed Neva. "I set the veronal there so—"

"You didn't!" snapped Kren. "I got the tablets out of the medicine cabinet in the bathroom, to fake suicide. Your uncle was choked to death. I did it."

"Why Kren—you couldn't have—"

"You heard him confess," gloated Devon. "Gotta get a cop here somehow." His eyes flashed to the street windows.

Neva cried, "Kren you didn't, I—"

"I did!"

Devon screwed his face up, said in a flat voice: "Make up your minds!"

He moved to the windows, reached for one to raise it. If a cop wasn't in sight he could call to a passer-by to summon the police.

Neva, her face white, eyes smoldering with fiery determination, suddenly pointed Devon's own gun at him. Her voice was a hiss of a snake ready to strike.

"If you call a cop, I'll plug you, Devon!"

The detective wheeled, shrugged rounded shoulders, his lips made a silly grimace.

Neva talked fast. "Get out of here, Treve. Beat it to your place. Benny's there. I let him in with the key you gave me. He's waiting for you. We'll tie up this nosey dick and—"

Out of the corner of his eye Kren caught a glimpse of the swift movement of Devon's gun hand. Kren swung up a chair, sent it hurtling through space.

Two guns boomed almost simultaneously.

The chair crashed against Devon's shoulder and the side of his head. Blood oozed from a scalp wound where a corner of the chair struck him. He dropped like a chunk of granite.

"The dirty rat!" cried Neva. "He tried to shoot me! But I got him."

Face set with worried lines, Kren bent over Devon, examined him carefully. Kren picked up his gat, put it in its holster.

"That chair I hoisted saved your life, Neva. Saved Devon's too. It spoiled his shot at you. Kept your slug, that tore through his coat tail, from getting him in a bad spot. The chair knocked him out for a bit. Scalp wound, but pretty deep."

Outside in the street voices were raised in excitement. Someone had heard the shooting.

Kren moved to the window. A whistle shrilled.

"People in the street are pointing up here. There's a cop running this way. We blow!" snapped Kren moving to the rear door.

Neva ran after him putting Devon's revolver into a dainty handbag.

CHAPTER VI

Death Stalks

TREVE KREN sat moodily in a westbound taxicab.

Neva spoke first. "Kren, I know you didn't kill Uncle. Why did you want to take the rap?"

Kren handed her the brooch he had found caught in the portières.

"Now you know. I saw you rush out of the shop and beat it in a cab about nine-thirty. I found Uncle dead. Devon tailed me there. He's certainly out to get me. The mug! Benny and I are going on the warpath tonight. We'll find out who crossed us on the Brewster deal. You got your bonds. Best you can do is beat it out of town."

"Got my bonds?"

"Cut the innocence," grated Kren. "I saw you go away with them tucked under your arm. A swell little crosser you turned out to be. I ought to cram my fist down your throat."

"Why—what do you mean?"

"That's a hot one! Why weren't you at the Viennese Café as arranged? You doped your uncle and squeezed his Adam's apple. Then you got your bonds and beat it. Why you came back, I don't know, don't care. All I want to do now is get the gink that put the finger on us for the Brewster—"

"You're nerts!" gulped Neva.

"Yeah? Well, I'm a sap to—mixin' with a dame that will pull the trick you did."

"Chump!" cried Neva. "When Uncle got back from Headquarters tonight he had a chill. Walking in the rain, his feet were wet, his clothes—he was chilled through. I put him to bed and made a hot toddy for him. He wanted the sleeping tablets so he'd get a good night's sleep. His nerves were all shot from worrying over things. Wilko phoned to tell me Benny was released because Brewster wouldn't press the charges. I left Uncle to go get Benny. I missed him at Headquarters and came back home thinking I'd find him there. I— I—"

"Go on. It listens swell," rapped Kren. "You told your Uncle that Benny was out. Demanded your bonds. Had a quarrel and croaked him."

"I didn't," cut in the girl. "I found the safe open and Uncle dead. I ran out and the portières fell behind me. I was too excited to notice my brooch had caught on them and pulled them down. I wanted to get to you as quickly as possible—to tell you not to go near the apartment—to tell you what had happened. You must have seen me as I left to go to you. I had my black pocket book under my arm. I forgot and left it in your place."

"With the bonds in it?"

"No. My God!" Neva's throbbing voice was almost a scream. "Who's got them? The same person that croaked Uncle must have them. Who could have done the job?"

Kren mused to himself. Without realizing it, he spoke just loud enough for her to hear. "Devon told me Benny threatened to get Uncle when he got out of the can—"

Neva gasped: "Benny! That kid! Well—maybe. He's my brother, but he'd cut my own throat for fifty G's. I see it now. I missed him at Headquarters. He went to Uncle's and did the job."

"You said he was at my place."

"Yes. I went to ask Dog-Face Bozan if he knew where Benny was," sighed Neva. "Benny was there. He and Dog-Face were having an awful row when I got into Bozan's room. Benny didn't want to come with me, but I made him."

"You told him how you had found your Uncle?"

"No—No! I didn't."

"You lie," Kren flashed angrily. "Now you want me to walk right in to my place with Benny sitting in the dark with a gat in his hand. Rub me out, then you can beat it with your fortune."

One small hand of Neva's flashed up to tear his face with her sharp fingernails. "You're nerts!"

"Mebbe. But I'm not crazy. You can cross me once, but not the second time. Gimme."

He snatched her handbag, took Devon's revolver and put it in his coat pocket.

IN the hall before he got to his door Kren paused, said to Neva, "You gotta key. Open up!"

The girl flashed a hateful glance at him, moved to the door. She called out softly: "Benny! This is Neva."

There was no answer from inside the room.

The girl turned the key, pushed the door open. A scream fled from her lips. She swept into the room, knelt beside a body sprawled on the floor.

Kren went in, closed the door.

Benny lay on the floor, his head in a pool of blood. He had been shot at close range. So close his right cheek was powder burned. The bullet had entered his right eye and come out through the top of his head. Benny never knew what killed him.

Kren's face went hard. Neva had said she had brought Benny here to wait for him. Was Benny alive when she left him? Or was he dead, like Uncle, when she fled from his apartment over the pawn shop?

He ran shaking hands through the dead boy's clothing. He found nothing of consequence. Benny's left fist was clenched tight. Kren gently pried it open. Blinked.

Neva collapsed in a dead faint. Two of her family wiped out in cold-blooded murder proved too much of a strain for her taut nerves.

Kren, for the moment, paid no heed to her. Intent was his gaze upon something he found in Benny's clenched fist. Benny didn't know what killed him. But he had known *who* was going to kill him. Carefully Kren removed several small strands of black hair from the cold hand. He put the hair in his cigarette case. Then he turned his attention to Neva, brought her out of her faint.

She sat up, tired eyes flashing fires of vengeance. "I know who put the heat on Benny. I know. Dog-Face Bozan! I'll bet he crossed you on the Brewster job!"

"What makes you think so? He hired us—"

"Didn't he beat it away from Brewster's last night when the cops showed?" argued Neva. "And tonight when I went to his dump he and Benny were fighting. If Benny croaked Uncle maybe Dog-Face *knew* Benny had the bonds—came here—killed him and got away with the swag."

Before Kren realized what her intentions were, Neva leaped to her feet, yanked Devon's gun out of his coat pocket. She said:

"You stay out of this, Treve. You thought I killed Uncle. Well, I'm telling you I'm going to mess up Dog-Face Bozan."

In her tragic grief, bordering on hysteria, Kren realized the uselessness of reasoning with her. He simply said:

"I'll tag along. You may need me to toss another chair."

Kren had ideas of his own. Dog-Face might have overheard Neva's plan and had planned to put over a fast one—rob Schulzer. Dog-Face probably went to Schulzer's apartment and caught Benny in the act of taking the bonds. Then in Dog-Face's room they had quarreled when Dog-Face demanded a split for his silence.

CHAPTER VII

Killer-Crosser

THE taxicab jounced over cobblestone paving in a squalid tenement district. Before a dingy, three-story brick house Neva called the driver to a stop. She and Kren got out.

A crowd of curious, awed people stood grouped about the rusty iron banistered front door stoop. A policeman stood guarding the front door.

"What's this?" Neva whispered.

"Wait," Kren said to the taxi driver.

He edged up to the crowd. Listened to the babble of hushed voices. "He's dead—shot right through the head—Naw, the eye, through the eye he wuz shot—I always said he'd come to no good—it wuz that gang he got in wid—the other cops otter be here by now—I heard the shot half an hour ago—Yeah? Well I called the cop didn't I?—He mighta been bad, but he wuz always nice to us neighbors—Yeh? Well I know—Dog-Face Bozan wuz a gangster—"

Kren didn't wait to hear any more. He strode back to the cab, said to Neva:

"Get in!"

"But—"

"I said get in. Dog-Face took a squirt of lead—Like Benny, right through the eye." He gave an address to the cabbie.

"Where you going now?" Neva demanded.

"Some place I should have gone first tonight."

"Where are my bonds?"

"Where I'm going."

"I don't get you."

"Well, it's my picnic from now on."

Neither of them saw a man rush from the crowd before Bozan's tenement house, get into a taxi and follow them.

NEVA, burning with curiosity, prodded Kren with questions. Finally he said:

"Someone put the finger on the mob. Benny and I were the new members. The Brewster job was our first. The mob had pulled a lot of profitable jobs. Someone was primed to wipe the mob out. First Benny is nabbed. Then your Uncle is wiped out. Next Benny; now Bozan. Both were shot through the eye. My job is to get the mug that's such a damned good shot."

"How's Devon with a rod?"

"That's sound reasonable," mused Kren. "He's not slow flashing one. I forgot all about him having that hunk of my coat. I should have taken that from him. Maybe it ain't too late!"

THE GOLDEN EAGLE, notorious South Side café in the rough-and-ready twenties, was a blaze of light outside. Inside, the lights were not so bright, shaded. The small hotsy-totsy joint was dingy. The underworld characters that made it their hangout wanted it dingy. Few that frequented the joint wanted their pans to be easily spotted by nosey flatties.

When the taxi pulled up to the curb, Kren got out, said to Neva:

"The picnic might be rough. You better go places."

She got out, stood beside him. "I don't know what's it all about. But I'm with you."

After Kren settled the bill they moved into the cellar joint. It was crowded with tables with red and white checkered table cloths. A grill and bar ran the full length of the room. There were no waiters. Customers got their food and drinks cafeteria style.

"Take a table," said Kren sweeping his eyes at the patrons that half filled the place.

"I said I was with you," retorted Neva.

They moved to the bar. Kren eyed a door at the rear of the room.

"Boss in?" he asked an oily faced bartender.

"You Kren?"

"Yeah."

"What'll it be?"

"Rye."

The oily faced man slid two glasses and a bottle along the mahogany bar top.

Kren poured Neva a drink. She took a sip, made a face and put her glass down. Kren tossed off a full pony. He glanced around the place. In surprise he noticed that the joint was nearly empty now. The customers had made an exodus for the front door. The few still in the joint were preparing to leave. To Kren this was a reliable gangland sign. The heat was about to be put on. None of the underworld joint frequenters wanted to be caught up in a police dragnet as witnesses to a killing.

"Boss in?" repeated Kren to the bartender.

The white-aproned man jerked his head toward the rear door. Let his hands slip under his apron.

Kren said: "Keep your mitts in sight on the bar."

The bartender shrugged, let his hands come up on the bar.

"Stay here, watch this bird!" Kren said to Neva.

She breathed: "If you're sap enough to walk into that room to get your belly full of lead, I'm going in ahead of you. I'll put a crimp in the play."

"Nothing doing—"

"Mama knows best."

Together they walked toward the closed door. Kren jammed a mitt into a bowl of potato chips at the end of the bar. Casually he tossed chips into his mouth as he strode to the door. Neva's hand got to the knob first. Kren shouldered her aside and bolted into the room. Neva crowded his back.

The room had a green felt-covered table and several chairs, a desk and a battered brass spittoon. The floor was bare worn boards. A barred window faced the alley near a door. Another door was in the left wall. A light glowed from a green shaded drop-light over the table. The room, thrown mostly into shadow by the shade, was empty save for the two visitors.

Kren closed the door, long-legged to the desk. He went through the desk drawers hurriedly.

"No bonds here!"

The door from the café suddenly opened. The bartender came in carrying a tray with a bottle of Green River and three glasses. He put them on the table. His oily features were an ugly leer.

"I wouldn't get nosey," he warned. He turned and went out.

A little gasp tore from Neva's throat. "A face. At that window there!"

Kren sped to the barred window, looked out into a black alley. Saw nothing.

The rear door opened and Bull Wilko came in banging the door loudly behind him. He didn't acknowledge the presence of Kren and Neva. He said in the voice of a tired man:

"Just been up making arrangements for Dog-Face's funeral." He immediately moved to the whiskey bottle. "Too bad. Young fellow, too."

"Only one funeral, Wilko?" asked Kren. "There were three murders tonight."

The whiskey bottle slid out of Wilko's hand. Thudded on the table top. He shot a sharp, surprised look at Kren. "Yeah? Who else?"

"Couldn't guess, could you?"

A sound of a car's motor purred somewhere along the alley, then stopped.

Wilko's right hand moved along under the edge of the table. He fingered a hidden push-button. Somewhere in the joint a buzzer dinned faintly.

"Riddle, eh?" he growled. "I remembered you said somethin' to Bozan 'bout his leavin' town in a box. What's the frail here for—to alibi you? Speak out. What's on your mind?"

"Uncle Schulzer, Benny, and somewhere around fifty G's in bonds," snapped Kren.

"More riddles," growled the big swarthy-skinned man. His eyes were smouldering black dots in a massive hard face. A big mitt pawed his hair back out of his eyes.

Kren whipped out his automatic. "Listen, Bull. You'll be a lamb before I get through telling you off. I got some black hairs that I took from Benny's clenched fist. They tell me you gunned him out. He made a grab for you and you plugged him. Why?—Because he must have gone home and saw you kill his uncle. Are those hairs worth the bonds you took from Uncle Schulzer's safe tonight after you phoned him that Benny was being released?"

Bull Wilko's lower lip dropped open. He tossed off a slug of whiskey. "A deal, eh? Oke. Show me the hairs."

"Show me the bonds!"

Neva, trembling with feminine rage, whipped out the revolver that belonged to Devon. She held it pointed at Wilko. Her words were bitter as gall. "You rat!"

Kren spat. "Uncle was the brains of your mob, Wilko. He fenced all your hot stuff. You needed heavy cash advancements for some phony deals you wanted to put over. A trick to rob him of his life's savings. He refused. You got sore. Then you got Dog-Face to get Benny into the mob. I smelled a rat, came in with Benny, figuring I was smart enough to play you one faster. You eavesdropped at my place and heard Neva tell me how I was to get her bonds. You got them. You killed Uncle, Benny, and Dog-Face—wiped out your mob to silence them. But I'm still alive. You're coming clean with this whole rotten game or you're going places—feet first."

Wilko smiled treacherously. "A deal's a deal. My hair for the frail's bonds."

"Right," clipped Kren. "Then we'll fight it out with gats. Either you kill me or I kill you for gunning out Benny, you louse! You got Bozan to hire me and Benny to do the Brewster job. You tipped us off to the cops or Devon. You wanted Benny to face a prison term to force Uncle to meet your demands for cash. And I'm going to kill you for being a sneaking rat!"

Beads of perspiration stood out on Wilko's wrinkled forehead. He pointed to a narrow clothes closet door. "The swag's in there."

Neva whirled, ran to the door. She yanked it open. A high pitched scream of terror wrenched from her startled lips. In wild-eyed terror she hurled herself to one side.

The bartender, crouching in the dark closet, swung up the short barrel of a Tommy gun. He had got into the closet from a secret panel at its rear. The vicious muzzle of the submachine gun was pointed at Kren's heart. The muzzle suddenly vomited a stuttering spew of orange-red flames. The room roared with the rackety-racket of the deadly gun belching hot lead at Kren at the rate of a hundred bullets a minute.

Kren dropped to the floor to the scant protecting shadow cast by the table. His automatic was sputtering fangs of flame as he went down.

Wilko whipped out an automatic. There was a sharp crack of a revolver. The gun in Neva's hand bucked, kicked out of her hand, thudded to the bare floor.

The bartender, blood spurting from his forehead, dropped head foremost out of the closet to fall across his hot Tommy gun. A slug from Kren's pistol had found its mark.

Kren staggered to his feet. His left arm hung limp, numb at his side.

Three spots burned in that arm as if red hot pokers were being skewered into his wrist, upper arm, and shoulder. A warm sticky fluid ran down his arm, dripped off his finger tips to the floor. In pain, weak from shock, he swayed on uncertain feet. He managed to turn to cover Wilko.

WILKO was not there. He lay sprawled on the floor. A deep red stain grew on his white shirt front. He had been shot just below the heart.

Neva cried: "I got the rat!"

The back door opened slowly, but Kren didn't notice. He got down beside the dying Wilko, rapped:

"You're washed up, Bull. By the dame you robbed and wiped out her family. I want you to know *that* before you cash in."

Wilko's lips wrenched into a ghastly grin.

"Uncle Schulzer caught me at his safe. I thought he was at the Viennese Café. He fought hard, I choked him. I was afraid Benny was wise I had crossed him. I got him at your place— Wanted to get you too. Bozan followed me, heard my shot that killed Benny. So I took him home. He wanted the dame's bonds to keep quiet. I let him have it. The bonds —in—in my—"

A shudder ran through his body. A bubble of blood swelled on his lips. And he was dead.

"My bonds! Where are they?" cried Neva.

Kren ran his hand inside Wilko's shirt. There was no heart beat. His wrist brushed against a bundle in Wilko's inside coat pocket. He tossed it to Neva.

"Here's your bonds. Wilko didn't have time to hide them."

He got up wearily. "What the hell?" He stood gazing incredulously into the leering countenance of Devon, head bandaged, standing inside the alley door.

"And a lovely time was had by all," said the private detective, with a sullen smile.

"So what?" growled Kren swaying toward him threateningly.

Devon clipped: "I didn't get all Wilko whispered. But I can tell the cops I saw the dame blast out Wilko and you put the heat on the bartender."

"Yeah?" challenged Kren. "I got the bartender in self-defense. You know that. Neva rodded Wilko when he flashed a gat. Now run along and collect the insurance company's reward for smashing Wilko's gang of jewel hoisters. They're all dead."

"Maybe I will," smiled Devon. "And maybe I'll tell the cops about *who* got Wilko."

"Maybe you won't."

"Who says so?"

"A slug in his brains that will tell the ballistic experts it came from your gat. You don't like that much, but you can't change it. Better play the good little hero stuff. Tell the cops you got Wilko in self-defense and for the good of your client."

Kren picked up the revolver from the floor and handed it back to Devon. Neva had an arm around Kren as he swayed out into the alley. They got into the taxicab Devon had waiting for him. As the cab drove away, Neva said:

"You're a honey to confess Uncle's out to save me—but what a chump!"

"Yeah," sighed Treve Kren. "When we get to a hotel room I'll send the cabbie back to collect the charges from Devon. That's not so dumb. A doctor won't be either, but I'll talk him dumb."